The Realities of Adoption

The Realities of Adoption

Jerome Smith, Ph.D.

MADISON BOOKS
Lanham • *New York* • *Oxford*

Published by Madison Books
4720 Boston Way
Lanham, Maryland 20706

12 Hid's Copse Road
Cummor Hill, Oxford OX2 9JJ, England

Smith, Jerome.
    The realities of adoption / Jerome Smith.
        p.   cm.
    Includes bibliographic references and index.
    ISBN 1-56833-090-1 (pbk. : alk. paper)
    1. Adoption—United States. 2. Adopted children—United States.
    3. Adoptive parents—United States. 4. Birthparents—United States.
    I. Title.
    HV875.55.S64   1997
    362.73'4'0973—dc21   96-53055

ISBN 1–56833–090–1 (cloth : alk. paper)

Distributed by National Book Network

⊖™ The paper used in this publication meets the minimum requirements of
American National Standard for Information Sciences—Permanence of
Paper for Printed Library Materials, ANSI Z39.48–1984.
Manufactured in the United States of America.

Contents

Foreword   ix
Preface   xi
Acknowledgments   xiii

1 Adoption: The Contemporary Scene   1
2 A Personal Note   9
3 Entitlement: An Essential Dynamic in the Adoptive Family   15
4 The Telling Process   29
5 Open Adoption: Boon or Bane?   35
6 Research in Adoption   45
7 Research in Open Adoption   57
8 Psychological Development of the Latency-Aged Child   69
9 The Adopted Adolescent   89
10 Transracial Adoption: Success or Failure?   101
11 The Birth Parents   107
12 Child Advocacy: My Role in the Baby Jessica Case   121
13 A Closing Note   131

Appendix   137
Bibliography   151
Index   157
About the Author   159

Foreword

It is indeed a pleasure to write the foreword to this timely and much needed book which will be of great benefit to everyone involved in the adoption process—adoptees, adoptive parents, birthparents, relatives, friends, and professionals. At the same time it is a special privilege to contribute to Dr. Smith's work, having greatly benefited from hearing his scholarly presentations and reading his very enlightening publications on the subject of adoption. He is a professor, researcher, clinician, lecturer, and writer of great renown, and his productions are always steeped in objective, well-documented clinical findings. He also brings a great deal of humanity to the field, speaking from the heart as an adoptive father.

The Realities of Adoption is a breath of fresh air in the rapidly changing world of adoptions. The pendulum seems to have swung from absolute secrecy and denial to unlimited openness with questionable closure. It is a time of chilling uncertainty as bitter custody battles gain increasing media attention, finalized adoptions are stunningly overturned, and infertile couples are flooding foreign markets to avoid these potential disasters. Dr. Smith brings to this atmosphere an air of calmness and insight that benefits all members of the adoption triangle. His articulate elaboration on the emotional and psychological process for all three parties is remarkable. With unusual clarity he defines the critical process of entitlement that adoptive parents must master to feel that "the child belongs to them unconditionally, and, perhaps even, exclusively." Regarding the increasing trend toward "open adoption," Dr. Smith portrays an objective review of current research and opinion, and while stating that the practice is highly controversial, he is clear on at least one point: "It is the adoptive parents who must be the child's psychological parents."

His illuminative chapters on how adoptees process their reality during different developmental stages, and on what might be their particular vulnerabilities, will be of great benefit to adoptive families and the professionals who may work with them. His respect for birthparents' struggles is a theme that adds a great deal of integrity to the book. While it is common for this part of the adoption triangle to receive little attention, Dr. Smith is uncompromising in his insistence that their feelings and needs receive the utmost consideration.

Aside from the overall thrust of the book as an examination of the contemporary realities of adoption, there are two chapters one will not find in other books on adoption. One is the focus on evaluative research, first in relation to adoption generally, then in relation to openness in adoption. Dr. Smith takes a middle-of-the-road position in guiding the reader through a deliberate problem-solving process in finding the delicate balance between clinical practice findings and understanding the various methodologies involved in this process. The other is the stirring account of his firsthand experience in the famous "baby Jessica" case. In this discussion, Dr. Smith's expertise as a child advocate comes through clearly; his stand for the welfare of this child never wavers, and society's response (or lack thereof) to the needs of children, he reminds us, is a yet-to-be-written chapter in the annals of human rights.

The major contribution of this book is the contention that adoption is a complex reality, one that must not be underplayed or overemphasized in family life. Dr. Smith does a remarkable job of presenting an even-handed and thoughtful way of dealing with issues that may arise because of it. Simply stated, this book is a most valuable resource for all involved in this family-building process.

Noreen M. Keenan, Ph.D
Albany, New York
September 2, 1996

Preface

My last work on adoptive parenting (*You're Our Child: The Adoption Experience*) was published ten years ago. Who would have thought that changes in adoption practice and the adoption experience itself would have witnessed such unprecedented variation from years past? After all, adoption practice as we know it today has been around a long time since 1851, if we judge the practice from the creation of the first adoption statute.

But that is the way it is. There have been many changes in adoption policy, all stemming from one basic premise: the assumption that adoption works best for all members of the adoption triad under a cloak of anonymity and confidentiality. And while research supports the view that the vast majority of adoptions work well, the field has been wrestling with the fact that there are many people out there, mostly adoptees and birth parents, who are acutely unhappy with the status quo.

I have felt for a long time that a new book was warranted that dealt with the controversies in adoption practice—including openness in adoption, transracial adoption, and the birth father movement. In the light of the recent openness in adoption practice and the proliferation of research material on this subject, I have felt very strongly that *You're Our Child* was somewhat outdated.

It was the publisher's desire to have me revise and update *You're Our Child*, feeling that its success in the past warranted a new version. But I believed that a book focusing on the controversies was more in order. Fortunately, we were able to craft a compromise, but one based on the realities of the practice. It was that thought that inspired me to name this work *The Realities of Adoption*.

Acknowledgments

There are many people who have provided me with support and encouragement to write this book. The first person who comes to mind is our daughter, Debra, who incidentally is our only biological child. I owe her thanks for spurring me on through its completion. The second person is my lifelong partner and best friend, Inez, who has suffered through the piles of papers and books in every room in the house. Third, are my two other children, Sandy and Bob, who really made me understand what adoption is all about.

There are a host of people who have made substantive contributions in the content. They are, and this is in no particular order of importance: Jennifer Hubbs; Courtney, Jim, and Ann Wottring; Elizabeth Mullett; Amanda Sutcliffe; and Erica Johnston.

I am grateful to Dr. Noreen Keenan for her thoughtful and helpful suggestions on actual content. Noreen and I have a bond in sharing the same dissertation chairman, Dr. Sheldon Tobin, from different institutions (hers being the State University of New York at Albany, and mine being the University of Chicago).

The typing of this book became the task of a very special person, Kathleen Hamlin, who shares my love of adoption. She is the mother of three children, including one who is adopted. Her painstaking efforts ensured that all that needed to be done in this book was actually achieved.

Finally, I would like to add a few words about people with whom I have suffered a loss in life. Loss is a key theme in this book, as everyone in the adoption triad suffers a loss, some actual, some fantasied, but no less real for this group. Actually, it is a matter of perception. If you *feel* you have lost someone, then you have, in fact, lost that person. And loss, with its deep accompanying hurt, is one feeling that we cannot overcome.

I would therefore like to dedicate this book to people whom I have lost over the years. The first is my father, Oscar Smith, who taught me the essence of life and the values contained therein. My mother, Anne Smith, nurtured me and taught me how to love. She recently passed away after a protracted battle with Alzheimer's disease. Though my siblings and I have been in a state of anticipatory grief for a long time, it will now be possible to go through a more normal (if there is such a thing as normal) grief process.

Finally, there are two other people whose friendships were so meaningful that they deserve unique mentioning. The first is Joan Connelly, a very special person who was summoned in the prime of her youth. The second is Susan Josephine Braun, also a young person, who I dearly miss and who taught me and helped me cope with loss in my own life.

To all of these people, let me say "thank you" from the bottom of my heart.

Chapter 1

Adoption: The Contemporary Scene

Say the word "adoption" and all kinds of mental pictures are conjured up. To an adoptee, the word connotes being part of a choosing process in the formation of his or her family. It may also connote a sense of having been abandoned or rejected. To an adoptive parent, it means that the rights and responsibilities of becoming a parent came through legal rather than biological channels. To a birth parent, it means loss and a giving up of rights attendant on becoming a parent. To the public, the word "adoption" represents the fulfilling of a double grace—the giving of a ready-made family to a needy child and a chance for a family to care for and nurture a child it otherwise would not have.

While definitions of adoption abound, my own preferred definition is "the permanent legal transfer of parenting rights and responsibilities from one family to another." The most important words in this definition are "permanent" and "legal." Technically, the word comes from the Latin word *adoptare*, which means to consider, to look at, to choose. From a practical standpoint, adoption represents a severing of the biological ties and a transference of the same rights and responsibilities to the adoptive parents. While it is a permanent arrangement, or at least is supposed to be, in practice it may not work out that way.

There have been cases in which a final adoption decree has been overturned at the request of adoptive parents, for a variety of reasons, but generally due to adoptee behavior problems of a rather severe and unexpected nature. What typically follows is a postadoption discovery that the information given about the child's background has been less than open and honest (usually in the case of an older child adoption). But there are other reasons as well. Recently, a completed adoption in Illinois (the well-known "baby Richard" case) was overturned by the Supreme Court in that state, creating havoc in this child's life. Because of this potential of reversibility, there are those who question the viability of the institution of adoption.

Adoption: An Institutional Response to Need(s)

I like to think of adoption as a solution to three interrelated social problems. The first is the problem of child dependency, involving children who are in a situation that does not provide the protection, nurturance, and ongoing care and love they need. Adoption provides this care by placing these children with people who have been determined to be capable, loving, and competent parents. Adoption also serves the purpose of dealing with unwanted pregnancies, in many cases teenagers not ready for parenthood, by providing counseling and placement services to the mother and family members. The counseling is directed toward helping her and the birth father to make a well-informed decision about the baby; should adoption be the preferred plan of action, the birth parents know that the child will be welcomed into a loving family. The third social problem is infertility. It is estimated that one couple in six faces this problem. Adoption provides these couples with a baby which otherwise would not have been possible. Thus, we have three interconnected problems—child dependency, unwanted pregnancies, and infertility, to which there is a mutual solution—adoption.

One cannot appreciate the contemporary view of adoption as an alternative family form without some historical perspective. From the earliest times, adoption existed in various cultures. The practice may not have been formalized through statutory provisions, as it is today, but there was recognition that children needed parents, requiring society to do what nature was not doing. A frequently heard statement is that adoption imitates nature. Adoption is a practice steeped in antiquity, certainly known in biblical times. Moses was, perhaps, the most famous adoptee. Our literature is replete with adoption stories, as mythical as Superman and as tragic as Oedipus. Children in need of protection and rescue are found in Oliver Twist and Hansel and Gretel (Brinich, 1990).

Historically, there have been varying views of adoption and its usefulness. For example, among the ancient Romans, adoption was viewed as a means of securing an heir in order to strengthen or extend a family line. In the Anglo-Saxon tradition, however, adoption as a legal arrangement did not exist. Neither the right to adopt nor the right to be adopted was known to English common law. In the United States, laws of adoption were introduced during the last half of the nineteenth century when the colonial practices of apprenticeship and indenture had become an inadequate provision for dependent children. Much social change occurred as this new nation became fully engaged in the transition from its simple agrarian beginnings to an urban industrialized society. This led to an increase in the incidence of child dependency, leaving the old, informal solutions of close family and community ties no longer feasible. As a result, new forms emerged to provide for children, of which adoption represented one. From those beginnings, adoption in this country has become the sociolegal process by which the parent-child relationship is established between people petitioning to adopt and the child to be adopted. The subject of the petition is almost always a minor child whose ties to the birth parents have been terminated by death, abandonment, relinquishment (most frequent cause), or by court decree (least frequent cause).

Adoption as we know it today is uniquely a creature of statute. The first adoption law was passed in Massachusetts in 1851. There is some reference to the state of Texas passing some form of adoption law in 1850, but generally, Massachusetts became the model for the remaining states. While American law developed from the English system, the concept of adoption required a new mechanism to institutionalize what was needed in America. Indeed, it was not until 1926 that England passed its own adoption law, some seventy-five years after the first American statute.

Over the years, adoption has been shrouded in myth. One of the earliest is the notion of an abandoned or orphaned infant needing rescue by a charitable couple. (Adoptable children are, in truth, rarely orphaned—in fact, in the social work literature, the term is rarely used. Rather, the term "social orphan" is used.) Reflecting the era's social Darwinistic notion of "fitness," adoption agencies developed the policy of the "blue ribbon" baby as the child most suitable for adoption. This policy necessarily led to agency practices that delayed placements until parents could be assured that the child was free of debilitating inheritable conditions. The myth deviates substantially from the realities of today but the attitude still persists that adoptive parents are rescuing a child from a life of blight and poverty. Furthermore, if the myth gets played out ("we rescued you") in the child's growth and development, the parents may well expect difficulties in conduct or behavior. At any rate, it is doubtful that this myth ever portrayed the realities of the typical adoption, and most certainly it has nothing to do with the realities of today. Recent years have brought a sharp decline in the availability of healthy white infants for adoption. The decline has been significant enough to force social agencies, up to now predominantly dependent on adoptions of infants as their principal professional service, to seek other service functions; such as specializing in placement of children with special needs. Today a couple may wait years to adopt, draining their economic resources. The tremendous inequity in the supply-demand ratio has forced couples to resort to extraordinary measures to bring to a birth mother's attention their desire to adopt. Advertising in Sunday newspapers is commonplace; some are even purchasing billboard space.

What has contributed to this change of placements decisions? First and foremost, society's attitudes about children have shifted from a "must place" to a "may place" philosophy. Because we are living in an era of greater sexual freedom, those unmarried persons who bear children are no longer considered immoral and most believe they should be permitted to parent their children if they choose to do so. The statistics relating to placement decisions reflect this attitudinal change. Before 1973, nearly 9 percent of all premarital births involved an adoption plan. Between 1973 and 1981, the percentage dropped to 4 percent. And for births from 1982 through 1988, the decrease continued, to 2 percent (Bachrach, et al., 1992).

This decrease is largely the result of declining percentages of white women placing their children for adoption. While the relinquishment rates for black women has consistently been low (less that 2 percent), nearly 19 percent of white mothers made placement plans prior to 1973, the same year the Supreme Court ruling in *Roe v. Wade* allowed abortions during the initial trimester.

Some experts argue that there is a connection between the decline in placements and *Roe.* However, the number of abortions leveled off during the 1980's while relinquishment rates continued to decline during this same period (Henshaw and Van Vort 1990), suggesting the influence of other factors, such as (1) an increasing number of pregnancies among unmarried women; (2) earlier sexual initiation among teenagers; and (3) peer pressure to parent. Collectively, these trends suggest changing attitudes toward single parents and a decrease in the stigma traditionally associated with such parenting. But very likely public awareness of the aftereffects of child relinquishment also contributed to this changed pattern.

Whatever the cause of this decrease, the effect upon adoptive parents is to eliminate the notion that they are the "rescuers." Ironically, they may instead feel that the child rescued them from a perpetual state of childlessness. Their long waiting period provides them with ample opportunity to make a deliberate choice to be parents; however, they do not choose their baby any more than biological parents do. If anyone is "chosen," it is the adoptive parents, not the child.

The traditional rescue myth still contains a germ of truth. Many children still await adoption—older children, children with mental and physical handicaps, children with behavioral disabilities, white or biracial children of all ages, and sibling groups. The adoption of these children poses substantially different problems than does the healthy newborn of the same race as his adoptive parents.

An extended discussion of these problems and proposed solutions is beyond the scope of this book. However, the existence of these children cannot be overlooked. Couples who want a healthy infant are advised that these other groups of children are available and subsequently may consider adopting a hard-to-place child. Although most choose not to undertake this special challenge, that they do consider it may contribute to a sense of having chosen their child. In this sense, adoptive parents do make a choice.

Both professionals and the community have become aware of this group of "special needs" children. These groups represent a new population of children for whom adoption has become a viable option because of notable changes that reflect altered attitudes in adoption policy. Services have expanded, and new concepts and principles are being applied in an effort to respond to the belief that these children are entitled to families. The definition of "adoptable" child has changed from the healthy, attractive white infant to any child who needs and could benefit from a loving family. Adoptive applicants previously evaluated by standards of childlessness and economic advantage are now considered for their capacity to nurture and parent. Strategies are applied such as recruitment, reduction or waiver of fees, transracial, single parent placement, and adoption subsidy, to try to achieve a more favorable balance between people willing to adopt and children waiting. Recognizing that adoptive families needed more financial resources, Congress has enacted a tax benefit. This is only one example of changes that benefit adoptive families and put them on relative parity with other families.

As a society, we have become more child-centered. Recently, *Dateline* (NBC-TV) told a story of an eight-year-old who, being removed from her parents' home due to poor parenting, including possible abuse, and forming a bond with her foster parents, was judicially returned to her biological mother. These events, all too common, point to a pattern of judicial decisions that ultimately favor the biological parents. After being personally involved in the high profile "Baby Jessica" case (which I refer to later in this book) and the "Baby Richard" case, I was not surprised that the appellate court ruled in this direction.

The public outcry is understandable as we witness these children being physically removed from their psychological parents. But what the public has to understand is that the "best interest of the child" is a myth. Rather, this concept comes into play only after parental rights are uncontestedly terminated in court. As noted later in this book, the rights of birth mothers and fathers take precedence over the best interest of the child.

We have witnessed many changes in adoption practice. In the early 1960s, I was a local administrator of a statewide statutory agency devoted to children's welfare (the Kentucky Department of Child Welfare). Because of the disparity between adoptive parents and available infants, the agency issued a public plea to recruit adoptive parents. Incredible as it may sound, the state had a surplus of healthy, free-to-be-adopted, Caucasian infants. We even had charts that looked like thermometers to show how each district office was meeting its goal (of x number of placements). Birth mothers at that time still felt the stigma of unmarried pregnancy, and saw no option other than placing their child for adoption.

Birth mothers were told in their counseling that by giving their baby up for adoption, they could put this chapter of their lives behind them, knowing that the child would be reared in a loving home. That they would get over their grief and sense of loss turned out to be, quite bluntly, a great big lie. In fact, most birth mothers continued to grieve the loss of their child, and thus the loss remained unresolved.

By the early 1970s, greatly aided by the ideological revolution of the 1960s, many changes took place in adoption practice. First, birth fathers were awarded (nearly) the same rights as birth mothers. Second, abortion was made legal, obviously preventing a number of potential placements. Third, transracial placement, which had increased in great numbers the previous decade, suddenly came to a near halt, when the National Association of Black Social Workers opposed such placements. The birth father and transracial issues will be dealt with in separate chapters. But the greatest change was that society relaxed its attitude toward single parenthood. The dual thrusts of the civil rights and feminist movements, as well as general unhappiness with confidentially oriented placements, provided the general framework for a new attitude toward adoption.

Today the pendulum has swung from confidential adoptions and moved toward greater openness. There are really three forms of nonrelative adoptions: confidential (the traditional anonymous adoption practice still offered by some agencies and attorneys); semiopen, or "mediated" (generally referring to a time-limited meeting between the adoptive parents and birth parents); and full disclosure, which dispenses with the anonymity secured in a confidential adoption. Openness in adoption is one of the most controversial issues and will be dealt with at length. I have altered my own view of openness since writing my previous book (Smith and Miroff 1987) based on two factors: (1) some preliminary research findings; and (2) the changing demands of adoption practice. But the reader should know that it will be years before we know how this new form of adoption practice affects children in any systematic way. That I needed to change my own views does not alarm me. What does alarm me, however, are the iconoclastic statements of experts in the field who call for an end to the practice of adoption, declaring flatly that it does not work and should be abolished (Baran and Pannor 1991). Such a statement belies the success stories of some 84 percent of adoptees (Kadushin and Martin 1988) and is tantamount to letting the small number of negative experiences cancel all positive ones.

I see no other field of practice in the social work arena that has gone through the (r)evolutionary changes that adoption has. Once viewed as an ideal solution for three interrelated social problems, adoption is now in question as a long-term answer. Adoption foes argue that adoption creates stress and trauma to birth parents and children alike, which are unameliorated by giving the children new homes and families. The time-honored arguments that permanent confidentiality and anonymity in placements are best for all parties are constantly under attack. Summarily, the assumptions we made relative to the best interest for all concerned are now being challenged, and challenged rather forcefully.

Finally, one should recognize that adoption is unique. As a parent-child relationship, it parallels in every way a procreative parent-child relationship. But its unique quality is that it creates a bond between adoptive parents and the birth parents. In effect, birth parents display an incredible amount of trust, trust that the adoptive parents will do all they can to justify by giving the child the love, care, and protection s/he deserves. The adoptive parents, for their part, promise to do their best to fulfill this responsibility while referring to the birth parents as decent, honorable human beings who made a tremendous sacrifice as an expression of love for their children. In the most successful adoptions, this contract is carried out quite well.

Chapter 2

A Personal Note

It may seem strange to my readers that I am including a personal reference to my work on adoption. I am, after all, a professor, clinician, researcher, and author. I should be able to distance myself from any personal or subjective account of the adoption experience. But as an adoptive father, I cannot. And I hasten to add that most of the theorists and experts in the adoption field today are themselves members of the adoption triad.

I grew up in a Jewish home, the second of four children (and the first male) to my immigrant Polish parents. My father was a sheet-metal worker who struggled to provide a home for his wife and children. My parents had emigrated to this country to escape the horrors in Europe, and my mother also left behind her parents and nine of her siblings (only one sister was able to leave.) Not until I became an adult did I fully realize the implications of that transmigration. As I was to learn later, the Nazis had overrun Poland when I was six and a half years old, to the day, and there is no doubt in my mind that I would have been destroyed in the process. Hence, I consider myself, in essence, a survivor of the Holocaust.

You may rightfully ask what this has to do with the subject of adoption. Just this—loss affects me very profoundly, and I always regretted never meeting any of my grandparents. I also want to visit Poland some day, to connect more directly with my roots. I know that adoptees have to deal with a loss, albeit an abstract one, but no less real to them. And thinking of the hurt that my two adopted children have had to face in confronting the reality that they were given up brings tears to my eyes.

My wife and I married in 1962 on an extraordinarily hot and humid day in August. At the time, I was a social work supervisor with the state of Illinois, working with children who had been declared by the courts to be either neglected and/or abandoned. They were, for the most part, "social orphans," a term used to designate a population whose parents were living, but otherwise so damaged that they could not act as parents. Their role as parents had been preempted by their personal problems, which directly affected their ability to carry out the parental role. I should state, parenthetically, that at that particular time, the state child welfare system in Illinois was open only to veterans' children, a carryover from the Elizabethan Poor Laws of England, in which certain classes of people were deemed more "deserving" of public resources than others. Not until 1964 was this requirement deleted.

But in 1963, my appetite was whetted for a new experience in social work, which coincided with my wife's desire to return to Kentucky, her home for the ten to twelve previous years. There was a job opening in the Lexington, Kentucky office of the Kentucky Department of Child Welfare. Even though I had no experience as an administrator, I saw this as an opportunity to provide some needed breadth to my professional resume. The primary activity of this agency was adoptive placement of infants. Much work needed to be done because restrictions on placements (such as religious matching) had been considerably relaxed. My job as district supervisor was to evaluate the family nurturing potential of applicants and to make the most appropriate match. (In those days, once a birth mother had requested counseling services, which may have included referring her to a maternity home, she virtually never decided to parent the child herself and the rights of the birth father were nonexistent.)

By 1965, my wife and I realized that we, too, were experiencing infertility, and we began to consider adopting an infant. We applied for a child with the Family and Children's Agency in Louisville, and on 6 July, a beautiful little girl was placed in our arms. Two years later, on my thirty-fifth birthday, a little boy was placed with us, and I recall deliberately not mentioning my birthday to the social worker, fearing that she might decide that we should wait another day. Such trust I had in social workers!

I had already begun to experience people's common attitudes about adoption. For example, when we brought Sandy, our firstborn, to my wife's aunt's home, she remarked, "Oh, she is so beautiful! How could anyone have given her up!" While I did not answer, I privately shared that same thought. But when our next-door neighbor remarked, upon seeing our son, that he and his older sister might some day marry each other, I rather indignantly responded, "I certainly hope not—they're growing up as brother and sister." My neighbor, realizing she may have offended us, replied, "Oh, of course, how silly of me!" What she was reflecting through her original remark was that, somehow, the incest taboo does not apply in adoptive situations—an extension of viewing adoption through a consanguinal lens. Another example comes to mind. When our son was a little leaguer, he was known in the tournament as the best pitcher. During the championship game, he pitched a perfect game, striking out all but two batters (who grounded out). In receiving accolades after the game, one of the parents (who knew our son was adopted) stated, "Of course, we knew of Bobby's athletic ability—he has great genes!" I wondered, hearing this, why I couldn't receive at least some of the credit for helping him develop his natural skills.

Just how deeply imbedded these attitudes were (and are) did not really come through to me until I began to read David Kirk's work, first in relation to community attitudes, and then in terms of how these attitudes affect adoptive families' feelings about themselves as "real" families (Kirk 1953; 1964). As the looking glass theory of Charles Cooley suggests, adoptive parents see themselves as a direct reflection of how others see them. Examples of these incidents are legion; people continually make such remarks without thinking. It is also important to recognize that such remarks are made independently of education or intellect. They revolve around the words "real, own, and natural." Adoptive parents who are unprepared, emotionally, to deal with the impact of this biologically determined chauvinistic bias have a most difficult time dealing with their hurt feelings arising from their own relatives' remarks. During my counseling sessions, I make it a point to confront adoptive parents on *their own* use of words which reflect this bias.

Zeroing in on the effects of these attitudes on involuntary childless adoptive mothers, a prominent sociologist discerned a perception that families formed by adoption were perceived as inferior to families formed through the procreative process, and that, further, the children were viewed as inferior (Miall 1987).

As an agency director whose primary business centered around the placement of healthy infants, I considered myself well informed about the rationale for certain agency policies. At our agency, we shared as much background information with prospective adoptive parents (all the nonidentifying information that we had in our history) as was available to us. Many came with pen and paper in hand. Some couples stated an indifference to such information—that should have been the tip-off that these folks were not ready to accept differences between biological and adoptive parenthood, a significant indicator, according to Kirk (1964) that something would go awry in the development of the child and the family. For example, when children want to know some facts about their genetic history, and they always do, it comes as quite a blow to learn that their parents know and are able to share very little.

It was also customary for families to listen to the background information, ask questions, and then go home to digest and work through the information. The child would be picked up the next day, per the parents' wishes, provided the social worker did not see signs of acceptance problems.

At the agency where we adopted our children, the practice varied somewhat. We were able to obtain background information and see the child, but would not be allowed to bring the child home until the next day. I remember thinking that night that "our child is in some stranger's home, and that's not right." Also, why the agency insisted on waiting five-and-one-half weeks between the birth and the date of placement, I'll never know. It was as if some kind of magic developmental milestone is achieved at this age. The truth is that we adopted our children during a time of transition. Delayed placements were giving way to more immediate ones, and the wait we had was obviously a compromise, albeit an arbitrary one.

The adoption costs were ridiculously low, especially by today's standards (somewhere in the neighborhood of $400). The attorney was a friendly man, and I recall that he said, as we crossed the street to the courthouse, "I like doing adoptions—everyone is happy. The couple gets a child, and the child gets a home." I realized this was the stereotype, but I remember asking myself, "but what about the birth mother, she's got to be sad."

The years passed. I had changed jobs, leaving the world of practice and joining the ranks of social work education. In 1970, I began my doctoral program at the University of Chicago, graduating in 1975. But throughout all of this, and having adopted not one, but two children, there was never a suggestion, or even a hint, from the adoption worker that adoptive parenting was different. And yet I knew it was.

Why, I asked myself, does our children's placement agency assume that adoptive parents know how to answer all the questions children ask about the birth process, about sharing information with them, and about why they were given up? While I concluded this was the norm, based partly on the placement practices of my own agency, I concluded that this was an area that needed some change.

Thus, I decided to offer courses in the community to adoptive parents that covered the following areas: sensitivity to the language of adoption; how to tell a child of his/her adoption; what adoption means to a child at the various stages of development; and dealing with one's own feelings about adoptive parenthood. The format of the meetings was lecture/discussion, and experts in various specialties were brought in, representing law, medicine, and genetics. It was during one of these meetings that a participant suggested that I write a book on the subject. This is my third such effort.

Over the years, I have seen many changes in the practice of adoption. The 1970s wrought many of these changes. No change has been more evident than the very fundamental assumptions under which adoption takes place. These are the idea that confidential adoptions best allow all members of the triad to go on living their lives in as productive manner as possible, and that adoption takes on no more, or less, significance than the color of one's hair or the nature of one's gender. That some people now challenge this assumption is why I wrote this book.

Chapter 3

Entitlement: An Essential Dynamic in the Adoptive Family

A long-standing view in the adoption field is that adoptive family life is akin to other ("natural") forms of family life, no more than a slight variation on the norm. Such a view presumes that adoption imitates nature, and that differences between the two forms of family life are virtually nonexistent.

There are those who claim that such a view is tantamount to denial, if not fiction, that it represents what David Kirk termed "denial of difference" (Kirk 1964), and that it in essence deceives adopted children during their formative years, with the result that these children feel victims of a plot to deny them of their heritage. The argument concludes that adoptees feel cheated out of something to which they have a right—knowledge of their birth origins.

How an Adoptive Family Develops:
The Stages of Growth

Multiple steps are involved in becoming adoptive parents. One must first recognize differences between becoming a parent as a result of a procreative process and becoming one through a legal process (steeped in misunderstandings, prejudice, and myths). As stated in a previous work (Smith and Miroff 1987), adoption cannot occur on an impulse. It is the result of a long process that involves mourning that leads to resolution. It cannot occur without an evaluation by an outside party. Its permanency is viewed as tentative particularly in the light of high profile cases in which children were returned to the biological parents, and it is invariably quite costly.

The right to parenthood is legally recognized in biological families, but adoptive families are required to go through a series of steps or stages, some external and others internal, before they become parents. The external ones are those set up by the state (agency, court, attorney, etc.) while the internal ones are those related to one's own feelings whether adoption is the right step and if one is ready to take it. (There is probably a middle group that is made up of neighbors' and friends' comments.)

These stages are referred to as "claiming" and "entitlement." They are both similar and different. Claiming is the process of informing others that we now have a child (e.g., birth announcement) who has been given this name (obviously more readily done for an infant than for an older child who recognizes his/her own name and identifies with it). Claiming also involves making a lifelong commitment to the child with all of the rights, responsibilities and privileges that go with this status (Anderson, Piantanida, and Anderson 1993). Entitlement is more complex and has to do with one's deepest feelings of the right of this adult to parent this child and the child feels that this is his/her family, This is the basic dynamic of an adoptive family. At the risk of oversimplification, claiming is a social process; entitlement is psychological.

The achievement of entitlement has been referred to in books and articles that refer to the adoption theme. I first came across this term in an outcome study (Jaffee and Fanshel 1970) of the relationship between adoptive parents and their children. These authors state,

> [T]he concept of entitlement emerged in our thinking as providing a useful perspective for understanding the dynamics of adoptive parent behavior. While the adopted child may be viewed as typically facing the task of resolving complex identity problems with respect to the two sets of parents who have played major roles in his life, we also considered it useful to think of a parallel identity challenge facing the adoptive parents. It was our conception that the typical adoptive parent is faced with the primary task of developing feelings of entitlement to his child.

While the concept of entitlement eludes simple definition, narrative or operational, this much can be said. Entitlement is the perception and the feeling that the child rightfully is yours. It is a response from both the head and the heart.

Entitlement means going beyond telling the child and the world that he or she is now yours. There are many feelings to contend with as one goes about this task of acquiring a sense of entitlement. Feelings of being different, being inadequate, that someone could have been selected as a "better parent" are manifold. The thought that someone else could do a better job as a parent (to this child) is an entitlement question. Margaret Ward states that "the sense of entitlement of the parents to the child, of the child to the parents, and the siblings to each other is a task unique to adoption" (Ward 1979).

One must understand that entitlement is a thought process, but it is more importantly a feeling. A feeling of entitlement refers to the parents' perception that the child really belongs to them, but that, more importantly, he or she belongs to them unconditionally and perhaps even exclusively. This is a relatively easy procedure when one has a biological child because there is no set of competing parents. So for biological parents, the sense of entitlement probably occurs unconsciously. Adoptive parents, however, must take that extra additional psychological step because they know that the child was brought into the world by another set of people.

Entitlement is an extremely complex phenomenon and some evidence suggests that it is not a question of whether or not one feels entitled, but to what degree one does feel entitled. Some parents will tell you that they have achieved entitlement when you ask them whether there is, in their minds, a set of competing parents. They answer invariably, "Yes, I know he is our child," but it has been my experience that in many cases, this is purely an intellectual response. Adoptive parents, being the intelligent group of people they are, are masters of defensive denial. Their feelings have been blunted, glossed over, or covered up with a host of self-reassuring statements such as "since we took care of Johnny since he was three days old, he is, therefore, our own child." Many adoptive parents have only developed a partial sense of entitlement, something we know because behavioral difficulties may manifest themselves in certain areas: problems with discipline; difficulty with allowing the child a measure of independence and individualization from the parents; or difficulty in discussing the adoption. It may also reveal itself in feelings of guilt that the child may never have access to full knowledge of his genetic past. A child's behavior problems may remind some parents of their infertility, resulting in overreactions of either rejection or overprotection (some parents find themselves in the untenable situation of giving the child material goods, extra allowance, cars, and so forth, thinking "this child has been rejected and it is not my right to bring additional difficulties into his life"). As parent-child conflicts become unmanageable, the parent may wonder if such behavioral difficulties are characteristic of all children at that age or if they are attributable, in some way, to the adoption. Some adoptive parents are vulnerable because they retain the uneasy feeling that the child is not really "theirs," in raising questions about whether or to what extent they are carrying out the proper parental role. Many experience a sense of role ambiguity.

Adoption expert Johnston correctly points out that entitlement is qualitatively different from attachment building, although the two concepts are inextricably interwoven (1992). If I had to venture a guess as to which leads to other, I would say that a family could feel attached to each other but not entitled. Entitlement, therefore, is the end result for a family that has successfully worked through their feelings of rightfulness to the child(ren), which includes forming an attachment.

Entitlement is also linked to a person's self-image. Where a person already doubts his worth as a human being, entitlement is harder to achieve. One example that clearly comes to mind is a woman who was forty-nine when she adopted seven-year-old Darcie, and expressed many feelings of personal inadequacy:

> I have always been obsessed with the thought that Darcie would not like or accept me. I was always afraid she would turn to me some day and say, "you should not have adopted me—the agency should have waited for someone else (younger) to come along." These fears turned into reality on many occasions.
>
> I was so fearful of this happening that I wound up giving in to her about anything and everything—even when my gut feelings told me to do otherwise. Then when her father and I got divorced, I felt even more guilty for taking the only parent she cared for (him) away from her.

It was obvious to the therapist, to whom this mother made these statements, that an internal struggle was going on inside this woman that made her question her right to parent this child. It was not the mother's age that was the problem— it was her feelings about her age. In the day-to-day interaction with Darcie, mother had to *continually* prove her worthiness.

In another case I recall vividly, a mother of two adopted teens and one biological teen was expressing how the adopted teens used adoption to their advantage. Whenever the adopted boy wanted something the mother refused to give him, he would counter with, "well, I can't expect it out of you—you're not my real mother anyway." Mother paused as tears rolled down her cheeks, to which I had commented, "and I suppose you gave into him at that point." She nodded her head in the affirmative. I then said, "Suppose your biological son said the same thing to you—that you're not his real mother. How would you have responded?" She unhesitatingly answered, "I'd say that's bull—," to which I answered, "there's your difference right there."

These two cases are similar but also different. Mother number one never felt that she deserved to be Darcie's mother, and she unconsciously invited the girl to use this fact against her. Mother number two did not have this same degree of self-loathing, but she did feel vulnerable to this form of manipulation. But both involve, to some degree, a failure to achieve a workable sense of entitlement.

Other cases too suggest the need for the couple to come to terms with the impact of infertility. Mr. and Mrs. K. had been married for five years and had one biological child when they learned that they would never have another. Mrs.

K. began to sob, whereupon the physician advised her to contact the agency immediately to initiate adoption proceedings. An infant was placed with Mr. and Mrs. K. within a matter of weeks. Years later the adopted child manifested many behavioral problems. The following is an excerpt from a meeting she and her husband had with me:

Dr. S.:   Do you feel that you have to compete with this other woman?

Mrs. K.:   The other mother? Absolutely. She was a threat to me from day one. Because I know how I feel about Raymond (my biological child), and I know how I feel about that birth connection, even though a lot of people in the group (of adoptive parents that had met several nights before) stated that there is no difference.

Mr. K.:   Don't forget that a lot of those parents' kids are too young to know what adoption is in the first place. Of course they don't have troubles yet—their kids aren't even at the talking stage.

Mrs. K.:   But I'm afraid. You know, I saw myself getting out there on that proverbial limb. I find myself getting these attacks of anxiety because there are things I want to say but I'm terrified to say them.

Dr. S: What would you like to say?

Mrs. K.:   I wanted to say, "I don't know how many of you sitting in this room have done it both ways. There is a difference and don't let anyone tell you otherwise. I don't have to worry about our own child, but for our adopted child, I'm scared that she is going to run away when she is sixteen. I'm scared that she is going to look for her [birth mother]."

Mr. K.:   I guess we're all worried about that.

Mrs. K.:   I'm terrified of that. I'm afraid of being judged. I'm afraid of her having to make a choice between two mothers, one who has made a lot of mistakes and some terrific mothers who never made any.

Dr. S.:   You know, she's going to have to find herself, no matter what.

Mrs. K.:   I know.

Dr. S.:   Maybe you're not seeing things realistically because your feelings
           are obscuring the reality. But when I spoke to your daughter the
           other day, there was no question in my mind that she feels she
           belongs to you. Now I don't know for sure if that was just a put-on
           or if she really understood the depth of my question, but I think she
           did. You're her parents. She knows that intellectually. But it's been a
           garbled kind of message. I hate to keep throwing up the nature of the
           message, but it's very important. What I mean is that if you're still
           competing with that woman out there, how are you going to
           demonstrate to your child that you're her mother if that competition
           is still brewing? The thing is—when you look at her, do you say,
           "You're my child?"

Mrs. K.:   Oh, absolutely. I always have. I mean it, I've never thought of her as
           being anything other than ours—mine, but on the other hand, I have
           to qualify that a little bit. I don't ever forget. I remember it, it's part
           of what she is. I remember that. You see, to me, I guess that's where
           the ambivalence comes from. That's part of her identity. She is
           adopted. That's what she is. To say that she isn't, or to forget about
           it, is foolish.

Mr. K.:   But I do. I mean, I've said to Jane—and never thought a thing about
           it at the time—Jane, you're a little fuss-budget, like your Grandma
           Miller. You're just fussing around all the time.

Mrs. K.:   I've said those things too, because those are her grandparents.

Dr. S.:   That's good.

Mrs. K.:   Okay, and I believe that. Those are her grandparents, they are the
           only grandparents we know anything about, or she knows anything
           about, but nevertheless, to forget it is senseless. She is adopted and
           one of the most pointed ways that we could ever even bring that
           subject up had to do with her name. I want her to have that.

Dr. S.:   I don't understand.

Mr. K.:   She was given the name Miriam by her biological mother.

Mrs. K.:   We had not picked out a name for her. When we went to get her that
           morning, a caseworker came out and was giving us background
           information and told us that the biological mother was seventeen

years old, said good-bye to her baby, and asked that this name be given to her. That's part of what makes it so hard for me. Because I do identify with her birth mother, and I know how hard it is to do— to give up that baby she carried for nine months, to know that somebody you're never going to see is going to drive up in a car and take this baby away from you, and that's it. It had to be devastating to her. And so we felt right then that we would honor her request and had it told to her. So that's why her middle name is Miriam.

Mr. K.:   That's the way it happened. But I would have never felt the need to keep that name. Why should we?

Mrs. K.:   I felt like we had been put through an ordeal, but that somebody was, out of her own pain, making up to us and giving us her baby. Anyway, when it comes right down to it, I don't think we have any right to her. That's why every time I see a TV show in which the birth mother shows up and says, "I want my baby back," it makes me so angry and so confused. I feel badly for both mothers. I mean, who does have the right?

Dr. S.:   It sounds to me like tremendous demands were placed on the two of you in caring for this baby. While I don't want to be critical of the caseworker, it's evident to me that a message was being given to you that the birth mother had a most difficult time in letting go. So your feelings of anguish, confusion, and guilt are quite natural, and I'm glad you got them out in the open.

Mrs. K.:   When I've really been horrible to Jane, I think about this seventeen-year-old girl, and I think about what if she knew?

Dr. S.:   What if she knew what?

Mrs. K.:   What if she knew that I treated this baby so badly? What if she wanted to come and take her away from me? (Sobs.)

Dr. S.:   Are you feeling that you somehow stole the baby?

Mrs. K.:   Sort of.

Dr. S.:   But the reality is that you did not steal or kidnap Jane. Whatever you have done to or for her, you've done in the name of wanting her to be the kind of person you believe she ought to be. Nobody said you had to be perfect. I would suggest that you examine your real feelings toward Jane and ask yourself if they would be any different if she were your biological child. But we place an inordinate standard of parental perfection on adoptive parents because of our belief that blood ties are everything.

Mrs. K.:   I have that hang-up with blood.

Dr. S.:   Well, you're part of our culture.

This case illustrates certain points: (1) Mr. and Mrs. K. did not have time to grieve the loss of their reproductive capacity; (2) they were ill-prepared for the differences between biological and adoptive parenthood; (3) Mrs. K. felt unusually competitive with the birth mother; and (4) the K.s' awareness of the difficulty that birth mother had in severing her ties with the child left them with a precarious uneasiness about their rights to the child. Obviously, the K family had not successfully worked through the issue of entitlement. Some aspects of their problems might have been alleviated by working through the feelings surrounding infertility and the differences between adoptive and biological parenthood. If this had not sufficed, it would be best for Mrs. K. to seek professional help to resolve her feelings and foster her sense of entitlement.

Varying, though strikingly familiar, theoretical models explain characteristic phases that couples go through before the resolution of painful feelings can be considered to be complete. One is the work of Elisabeth Kubler-Ross, whose characterization of the mourning process is particularly helpful in understanding how couples deal with the impact of infertility (1969). These phases of mourning entail an extremely lengthy process, which cannot be rushed. For adoptive parents, an understanding of these phases is imperative.

Ample evidence suggests an identifiable association between the resolution of infertile feelings and family functioning. Unresolved feelings of disappointment, anger, or guilt about infertility can have a powerful effect on family life. Couples may perceive infertility as a deprivation or even as a loss. If they fail to come to grips with such feelings the result may be an atmosphere of tension for the adopted child and the family as a whole. Elizabeth Lawder's research (1969), in which she examined the relationship between adoptive outcome and attitudes toward infertility, suggests that the ability of the father and mother to accept infertility does have a bearing on the acceptance of the adopted child and hence, on the child's later functioning. She states:

> The adoptive mother's ability to discuss infertility prior to placement was significantly related to outcome. Although the father's ability to discuss infertility showed a relationship to parental functioning, the degree of relationship was consistently smaller than that from the mother. . . . The association between the

mother's ability to discuss infertility and parental communication of the fact of adoption to the child suggest that the better the parents understand these feelings the better they are able to cope with the related problem of telling the child of his adoption. (167)

Again, I need to stress that it is not the infertility that is the critical variable, but the feelings that result from missing the opportunity to produce biological offspring.

Actually, our knowledge of how couples react to the news that they will remain childless is rather sparse and based on limited data. In general, however, they react as they would to any severe crisis. Families characteristically go through several phases in accepting infertility. The phases vary in length with each couple and tend to overlap with each other (Mazor 1979). They consist of (1) a period of denial; (2) anger and grief reactions; and (3) acceptance.

During the first phase, many couples deal with their feelings of disappointment by denying the reality of the situation. A characteristic response is "not us." To prove their fears are indeed wrong, many couples go through medical procedures and tests, some physically painful and some psychologically demeaning. Some people react with a sense of helplessness at losing control over their life's plans. In my experience people who truly value their own autonomy and sense of control over their lives experience considerable difficulty accepting the reality of this one "flaw." Other individuals may go through a bargaining phase during this period, in which they offer to suffer in return for a baby. Such bargaining is exemplified in the biblical account of Hannah, who promised to give her son (if God granted her wish) to the Lord all the days of the child's life (1 Samuel 1:11).

During the second phase, denial is replaced by anger as the couple now asks "why us?" They may feel an extreme sense of injustice, as if they had somehow been singled out. Couples may question which partner is "at fault" and begin to doubt the security of their marriage. The experience produces a sense of failure in some people. Even couples with good relationships and strong marriages may experience these feelings of insecurity and failure, at least temporarily. Typically one spouse may remark to the other, "if you had married someone else, you would have a child by now." The feeling that one has betrayed the bloodline as well as the spouse is difficult to counteract.

In part, this reaction is linked to our cultural expectations, and in my experience is more likely to involve the woman. One frequently heard remark is, "You're not a woman until you have had a baby." In addition, in our culture at least, women are considered the adult family member most responsible for maintaining family ties. Some signs point to changing societal values that give men and women shared responsibility. However, attitudes still give men primary responsibility for maintaining the family financially, while women remain keepers of family ties at home. Some men may experience a sense of failure for not carrying on the family name. Another reaction, culturally derived, is the feeling that one does not deserve to enjoy sex since the act isn't producing a baby. Again, this derives from sexual mythology and in some cases religious beliefs that state that the sole purpose of sex is to procreate. This perspective is changing, but there is always a time lag between changing ideologies and our inculcation of them.

Couples experience grief and mourning, as well as anger, with considerable intensity during the second phase. Many couples report, however, that the mourning experience during this phase has brought them closer than before. The couple able to acknowledge such feelings soon develops a desire to handle them through discussion with each other or professional counseling. Feelings of inferiority can be alleviated by restoring confidence in parental capacity, by a hope that one can continue to satisfy the partner emotionally, and by the recognition that sexual competence and reproductive powers are not synonymous. It is important to recognize that this is a process of working through feelings over time, and that old feelings—of inferiority, failure, and incompleteness—are not easily dissipated. One must keep comparing feelings with the intellectual understanding of the situation, and occasionally ask oneself, "Is this feeling reasonable and how much is it truly tied to the reality of the situation?" The answer may be a long time coming. The main thing to remember is that it does involve *a process*, a working through of feelings, and that mutual supportiveness of husband to wife and vice versa is essential, regardless of who is "at fault."

Some couples may feel themselves "stuck" in the anger phase. For infertile couples, the anger is most frequently a response to the helplessness and loss of control over life's plans, hopes, and goals. In an effort to regain control, many become preoccupied with timing sexual activity to coincide with the period of anticipated ovulation. The desperation and artificiality associated with sexual activity often are unrecognized sources of anger for those couples who once enjoyed sexual spontaneity (Shapiro 1982). As the goal of sexual intercourse shifts from pleasing partner and self to the fertilization of the ovum, or the process to results, feelings of hopelessness and anger inevitable result. Many couples learn to avoid love-making because it is not being the "right time," and indeed, many experience a loss or weakening of the sex drive itself.

A period of depression sets in when the couple realizes that no amount of diagnostic workups, regardless how specialized they may be, no surgical intervention, and no amount of bargaining will change the basic fact: there is a high degree of improbability that pregnancy will occur. Together, the couple must come to terms with the loss of their reproductive powers and mourn the loss of the child they'd dreamed of having. It is truly a difficult task because the loss is so vague—no formal funeral ritual acknowledges it. Also, people can be quite insensitive to the pain experienced—some even to the point of joking about how much fun they can have trying again. The loss may be mourned again on many occasions, for the world is full of reminders that other people continue to have babies, but the pain becomes less acute with the passage of time. In a sense, learning to live with infertility is akin to learning to live with the reality of death—it is part of life.

The final stage of working through the feelings is acceptance. In this stage the pair comes to terms with the situation that they face. This presumes that the couple realizes that while they may not propagate children in a biological sense, life is full of other rewards and satisfactions. However, during this stage, they may have a renewed desire for a child, and the compensatory wish to give of oneself (to a child) becomes stronger. Finally, couples who cannot procreate realize that they can find enormous satisfaction and fulfillment in contributing to a child's growth and development even if that child is not "born" to them in a physical sense. It is not procreation that makes one a parent, but the sense that one is contributing meaningfully to the life and self-actualization of another human being. Of utmost importance to the couple's ability to achieve a comfortable level of acceptance is their ability and willingness to share their feelings and recognize that they are normal.

Couples should be aware of their feelings about infertility so that unresolved emotions will not cause problems with family relationships and functioning. How does a couple know when they have resolved such feelings? In general, when they can discuss adoption openly, generally answer questions about the adoption without defensiveness or resentment, and talk about adoption with the child at appropriate times all indicate a relatively healthy resolution.

It is relatively easy to detect failure in resolution. Some of the many possible indications are: prolonged denial of feelings of disappointment; sadness, or resentment in observing a pregnant woman; reacting with annoyance or irritation to "normal" children's play; avoidance of family reunions where children are expected to be present; obsessive fears that the child will not measure up to family standards; anxiety about discussing adoption; repeated joking remarks about the similarity between the child's and (adoptive) parents' looks and/or behavior; bringing up the child's adoption under virtually any circumstances; feeling compelled to tell the child how the parents "took him in" at varying points in the child's life (the rescue notion); fantasies about one's imagined biological child; a persistent, nagging feeling that one was cheated, leading to a "not fair" response; and unabating resentment toward visits by the agency social worker.

While this list is not exhaustive, it does represent the kinds of situations that reflect gross uneasiness about feelings related to infertility and hence adoption. Some of the responses fall into the denial category; others fall into the angry or "why us?" category. Most important however is, that adults *be aware of their feelings,* even if those fears seem irrational, and be prepared to discuss them with a spouse or professional mental health clinician.

Because of the stigma generally associated with mental health counseling, many people are loath to seek it out. That one needs such services should not be interpreted as a perceived defect in one's psychological armor. There are two types of assistance available. Individual counseling by one trained in helping couples deal with the special psychological tasks can lead to a greater sense of entitlement. In many cases, they must work through feelings that previously blocked a healthier adjustment. Groups on adoptive parenting can also be helpful. Group discussions provide a means for parents to talk about and reveal the myriad ways that each couple deals with life and growth problems. Besides revealing problems, the group discussions demonstrate how gratifying the trying out of new experiences has been and how their lives have changed. Couples need to know that others also struggle with the special problems preparatory to adoptive parenthood, and may be comforted by seeing that these struggles do not make them poor parents or any less the parents of their children.

There is a practical matter to be considered in the timing of adoption inquiries and application. In the past, I have advised counseling people not to adopt until they have more or less successfully dealt with their feelings about their childlessness. This was good advice when healthy babies were plentiful, and the wait was relatively short. But today, when couples are required to wait from four to six years after they apply, it doesn't make sense to prolong the wait more than necessary. Therefore, I feel it is appropriate to consider adoption while working through the feelings described. Presumably, by the time the placement is made, the feelings will have been resolved.

Once adoptive parents adjust psychologically to their unique situation, they can go on to tackle the other factors that interfere with their attempts to obtain a comfortable sense of entitlement. They still must confront the task of dealing with the societal attitude towards the institution of adoption—attitudes that emphasize the differences between the two types of parenthood, and that convey only conditional acceptance of parenthood through adoption. This societal ambivalence is reflected in our patterns of speech and mores. Consider one of our best known axioms: "Blood is thicker than water." Such views lead to a certain defensiveness in adoptive parents, who are expected to respond undefensively to remarks from relatives such as, "Now maybe you can have one of your own." People who make such tactless remarks obviously do not realize the prejudice these remarks contain nor their potential to hurt.

Consider, also, the terms we use in describing birth parents: "natural", "real", and "own." This may imply that adoptive parents are somehow unnatural or unreal or that parenthood by adoption is an inferior form of parenthood. Yet these terms continue to be used, not only by the public, but also by professionals in the field, seemingly unaware of the biological chauvinism they are fostering.

Even some apparently positive attitudes contain seeds of doubt about the legitimacy of adoption, as in the choice of words of well-intentioned friends who continue to emphasize the difference of this form of parenthood. Undue congratulations containing subtle messages are heaped on the couple. Remarks like, "How lucky for the child to have parents like you!" are not infrequently made. Many remarks reflect the rescue fantasy by implying that the child, perhaps the product of a union between "inadequate" people, is rescued from a life of blight and neglect. Such remarks would rarely, if ever, be made to parents following the birth of their child. In fact, one would more likely say to new (biological) parents, "How lucky you are to have such a beautiful child!"

In an interesting study of community attitudes toward adoption, Kirk (1953) found that nine out of ten couples heard such remarks as "Isn't it wonderful of you to have taken this child!" and "This child looks so much like you that he (she) could be your own!" Four of five were asked, "Tell me, what do you know about the child's background?" One out of two parents was told: "He is a darling baby, and after all, you never know for sure how even your own will turn out." One out of three heard: "How lucky you didn't have to go through the trouble of pregnancy like I did." Finally, one out of five heard: "How well you care for the child, just like a 'real' mother."

Adoptive parents should realize that it is not necessary to passively listen to such remarks. Since people do not intend for their remarks to hurt, it is reasonable and appropriate to correct these "well wishers." A question such as "what do you know of the child's parents?" should be responded with "what would you like to know about us?" Through the uncomfortable few moments that follow comes a greater appreciation of just what adoption means to the adoptive family. The same advice is suggested for the words "real," "natural," and "own." Such handling of these seemingly innocent and tactless remarks will have the effect of a public education effort, which, in turn, will reduce the tendency of uninformed people to say similar things in the future.

The problem with the word "real" is that it suggests a comparison, usually of an invidious nature. Once you label parents as real (biological), you ipso facto suggest unreal or false parents (adoptive). This can directly affect adoptive parents' feelings of rightfulness to the child. In this case, many parents feel the need to prove they are fit parents, and frequently attempt to do so in outlandish ways (e.g., buying the child everything s/he desires), leading to an overindulged child with the problems associated therewith.

On the other hand, adoption is often viewed in positive terms. People who adopt children are congratulated by relatives, friends, and other well-wishers. Baby gifts are sent and the entire occasion is recognized publicly. Some parents even send announcements, modified to reflect the nontraditional way the child came into the family.

Entitlement is a psychological task for the adopted child as well. Many hear remarks from friends, neighbors, and family about one's looks, who does he or she favor, and these questions, comments, and remarks do affect the thinking and adjustment process. A struggle, therefore, goes on in an adopted person's mind that relates to the question of "who am I?" I will take this up further in the chapters on latency and adolescence, but I want to comment on it briefly as an entitlement question. So if a teenager says, "I don't belong to this family," or "this is not my family—I'm adopted," the entitlement has not been worked through. When a twelve-year-old says to his mother, "You're not my 'real mother,' I don't have to listen to you," and mother feels powerless in responding, it affects the entitlement on both sides. So the real test of entitlement comes, not from dialogue between neighbors and friends, but in day-to-day interactions between parents and their (adopted) children. When the adoptive parent refers to the birth parents as "real parents," entitlement has failed. When the child says, "This isn't my real family," entitlement has failed. To sum up, a family is a feeling and your "real" family is the family you feel is your "real family" regardless of blood ties.

Finally, one must consider how entitlement works in open adoptions. There are two ways to look at this. Those arguing for a continuation of the confidential form see entitlement as being diluted, since the openness, especially in full disclosure, brings into sharp focus the other set of parents and can diminish the sense of entitlement necessary to the child (Watkins and Fisher 1993).

McRoy and Grotevant (1994) found no basis for this fear. Reitz and Watson (1992) go even further in stating that "open adoption procedures in which the birth parent has some voice in the selection of the adoptive family or even hands over the child to the new family are powerful entitlement experiences." Openness in adoption will be handled in greater detail in subsequent chapters.

Chapter 4

The Telling Process

As I prepared to write this chapter, the thought crossed my mind that advising people how to go through the telling process was a relatively simple task in a traditional confidential adoption. In that form, the child views the birth parents from a fantasy perspective. They found themselves in a situation in which they felt themselves not to be ready, materially or psychologically, to be parents, and so asked the agency to find the most suitable parents of their unborn child. When the adoptive parents speak of the birth parents, the child imagines what they look like, what they are like as people, why they decided as they did, and so on.

I plan to recap the advice given for such placements because this may still be the norm in many settings. But since openness, in some form, is a reality at the heart of placements, telling must take on a different form. This includes, of course, not only the process through which the birth parents decided on adoption, but how the adoptive parents should refer to them.

First, a few comments about telling in general are in order. The telling is a unique aspect of the adoption process, and for some parents, it is still quite troublesome, depending on the degree to which they have achieved entitlement. (Varying research findings only further complicate the picture. Brodzinsky states that this is a troublesome area for adoptive parents [personal communication] but my research findings suggest that parents are actually looking forward to the event.) If the adoptive parents are still struggling to develop feelings of entitlement and are uncomfortable with telling the child about an original set of parents, the child may well respond more to the parents' anxiety than to the content they mean to convey. Finally, through the telling, the parents must explain why they needed to resort to adoption in the first place. To the extent that the telling stirs up angry or resentful feelings because of unresolved feelings about infertility or sexual adequacy, the spontaneity and warmth recommended in the telling may be severely compromised.

It is my view that parents need suggestions on various ways in which to tell their child of the adoption; I do not think that they should be led to believe that there is only one right way to tell. In the adoptive parent classes that I offer, between 80 and 90 percent of the couples pose this concern as the primary motivating factor for taking the course. It is also my experience that parents are often needlessly anxious and concerned about the child's reaction and ability to handle the "news." Such anxiety may reflect the parents' projection of their own discomfort and lack of coping skills. If the parents have worked through their feelings about whose child this really is, the "homework," in a sense, has been done.

When the child asks, "Where did I come from?", it is important to answer his question openly and without hesitation. I view the telling as a very important time in the child's lifespan and development—a special moment, if you will, between the parents and the child. I liken the importance of this special moment to a proposal of marriage, or the actual marriage rite, in which two people commit themselves to a lifelong bond. It is conceptualized as a happy moment—one that will always be remembered with positive feelings. The telling can be a most gratifying experience—one that adds to, rather than detracts from a feeling of belonging and identity. Instead of perceiving the occasion as a threat to the parent-child relationship, parents should view it as a challenge and as a way of solidifying a positive bond. Research findings confirm this view: The more open the subject of adoption, the better the child's adjustment to it (Witmer 1963).

One should remember that all families have rules. In some families, these rules are explicit, in others, implicit; that is, all family members operate as if they are explicit, but just don't talk about them. The subject of adoption may be an overt or covert rule to either immediately launch into or avoid, at all cost. Either approach is a decided mistake, in my judgment. In other families, there may be a rush to judgment about a problem unrelated to adoption (e.g., dating), and the parents jump on the adoption theme, making it the scapegoat. Either approach, the avoidance or attack, is bound to create problems or exacerbate existing ones. When one looks beneath the surface and uncovers a parent's avoidance of parental responsibility, it can lead to a sense of tentativeness about the relationship on the part of the parents, the result of alienation and aloneness (Watkins and Fisher 1993).

There is one basic principle that I believe all adoptive parents should understand and adhere to: the ease with which the child fully accepts his status relates directly to the degree of the adoptive parents' success in accepting (and feeling entitled to) their own status as adoptive parents. Several clues may signal the degree of such acceptance. If the parents can discuss adoption openly, without fear, guilt, or embarrassment, rather than either avoiding the topic or feeling the need to reveal it with every conceivable opportunity, it indicates that they have accepted the situation. If, on the other hand, they are struggling with fantasies of how their own biological children might have looked and behaved, or react emotionally or defensively to the news of a friend's pregnancy or the birth of a friend's child, the underlying attitudes need to be more fully explored. Under such circumstances, discussions about adoption may take place at inappropriate times and convey to the child a sense that something is wrong. *Either too much talking about adoption or not talking about it at all indicates that there are problems in acceptance.* Parents should also realize that children respond more readily to feelings and nuances than they do to what is being said. They are particularly tuned in to feelings, even feelings about which the parents themselves may not be particularly aware.

The "telling" has undergone some shifts over the years because it remains unclear how children adapt to the news of their adoptive status. A phenomenological issue is at stake here: some adoptees view it, at least consciously, with a sense of pride, saying, in effect, "I'm glad I'm adopted—it makes me feel special." Others see it as a burden, a stigma, a family secret, which renders them vulnerable to peer attacks that "your 'real' parents didn't want you. You're a reject." One eight-year-old adoptee told me, with considerable consternation, "Why should I let others know I'm adopted—they will have ammunition I can't defend myself against." But while professionals may disagree about the effect of the telling in children's lives, I view it necessary to stress a point that has the full backing of my clinical experience and is compatible with documented case studies. It is simply this: When adoption is poorly handled in a family, it is not the fact of adoption that makes for emotional disturbance but something more basic. It has to do with the nature of relationships with a family, and whether people are open with each other and caring about each other's needs. It has to do with the openness or closeness of communication and whether it is honest and trustworthy or rigid or dishonest. It has to do with loving and caring feelings, or the obverse, cold and highly critical ones. It is how a family communicates. It is simply the general dysfunction in a family that disturbs a(n) (adopted) child, not that he or she is adopted.

Consider the following case. Mr. and Mrs. R. were an older couple who had adopted Keith when he was four days old. Mr. R. had a very successful career as a building contractor and Mrs. R. was a retired teacher. The placement was effected when the R's were forty-nine and forty-eight, respectively, considerably older than the norm. They had already adopted one child, William, when the caseworker showed up at the house unannounced, holding a scrawny, obviously sickly child, and asked whether they would keep the child for a matter of weeks until an adoptive placement could be made. The R.'s accepted the challenge and did not think that this would pose a problem for their eight-month-old William. Keith was never removed from the home but subsequently adopted by the R.'s. In time, they adopted a third boy, although this placement was by design, not happenstance.

Over the years, Keith began to exhibit serious behavior problems. Although of normal intelligence, he failed all of his school courses and engaged in lying, stealing, and fighting. He did not feel close to either parent and frequently felt scapegoated by his two brothers. (The parents invariably took the other boys' side in a sibling dispute.) It was clear that every member in the family lined up against Keith and told him that he was "the weird one, the oddball, the one with the problem." By the time Mrs. R. brought Keith in for therapy, the hostility and sense of alienation had become irreversible. One particular message Keith reported hearing whenever a conflict occurred between Mrs. R. and Keith, and she was clearly disappointed in him, she asked (him) if that was the treatment she deserved for taking him in and, in effect, rescuing him. Keith expressed to me how angry these remarks made him.

Again, it is not the adoption itself that makes for the good or poor adjustment, but how it is handled within the family. Had Mrs. R. not managed conflict situations by resurrecting the adoption issue, the problems might not have been as severe as they were. (Genetic predisposition may have been a factor as well.)

Social agencies tend to take a position of openness about adoption from the very beginning of a child's life. They commonly instruct parents to begin to tell the child of his adoption as early as possible in his development and certainly before he enters school. The child is to be told of his chosenness to diminish any tendency to think of himself as unwanted (by the birth parents). This practice not only eliminates a potentially traumatic experience for the child who suddenly learns of his adoption through the careless and insensitive remarks of friends and relatives, but also provides the child with the opportunity of integrating the "adopted" self-image into his thinking from the beginning.

Extending the principle of openness to contemporary practice, one sees many variations, and the principle of honesty and forthrightness with the child still applies. But as one moves from a confidential form of adoption to the gradations of semiopen and finally, full disclosure (identifying information given), the birth parents become less figures of fantasy and more real persons. But regardless of the openness of the placement, the adoptive parents must present a realistic picture of the birth parents and help the child integrate these real people into their lives and psyches. In the case of full disclosure, I would abandon my previous advice of referring to the birth mother as "birth lady" as this is too much a sugarcoating (that the child could see through anyway)—call her the "birth mother."

While the field is unable to state, definitively, how this new practice affects children, it may indeed cut down on the sense of loss and discontinuity. As summarized by Anderson, Piantanida, and Anderson (1993):

> A distinctive, yet normal process for these families involves clarifying the extent of openness and the nature of the relationships among birth and adoptive family members. When members of the birth family have ongoing involvement in the child's life, it is incumbent on all parties to work constantly to make these complex and unusual relationships understandable to the child.

Yet the shift from telling very little about the birth family (usually the demographics of height, weight, color eyes, educational level, perhaps health status) to everything may carry some unintended consequences. For instance, a number of years ago I visited a family in Green Bay, Wisconsin, who had adopted under a full disclosure arrangement in which the two adoptive brothers had different visiting arrangements with their respective birth mothers. The boy whose birth mother chose not to visit became visibly upset whenever his brother's birth mother did visit. Many of these arrangements will require continued involvement with the agency worker, who may need to give special attention to a particular child. A number of different scenarios are played out in a realistic portrayal of these changes in practice (Melina and Roszia 1993).

In summary, telling the child of his adoptive status is regarded as the single important task in the (adopted) child's psychological development. Although professionals disagree about the timing of the telling, the research findings repeatedly show that delayed telling is associated with heightened negative reactions on the part of the child (Witmer 1963; Triseliotis 1973). Parents may need some help in formulating the technical aspects of the message, but if their feelings for the child are love and warmth, the particular words used are of little consequence. The ease with which the child accepts the news of his adoptive status is very directly related to the comfort level of the parents in accepting their own status as adoptive parents.

Chapter 5

Open Adoption: Boon or Bane?

Adoption, at times, takes strange twists. Adoption was originally conceptualized as beneficial to all parties in the triad: adoptive and birth parents and adopted children. Agencies considered it sound practice to share non-identifying information with the adoptive parents, who, in turn, would share such information with the child, in appropriate doses, and at ages consistent with his/her developmental needs. The secrecy surrounding identities was considered in the best interest of the child. A birth mother was assured that she could put the pain behind her, close this chapter of her life, and take comfort in knowing that the child she would relinquish would be provided with a loving family. Adoptive parents would become the legal parents and assume all the rights, responsibilities, and privileges accorded biological parents. This anonymity was symbolized by the sealing of records under the control of the agency and the courts. To buttress the view that the adoptive family should resemble a biological family as much as possible, the placement system appeared to minimize anything that made adoption different from biological parenting (Bradshaw 1995). Within the system the idea that something was wrong with this arrangement was not yet born. Likewise, the idea that birth parents would literally choose the parents of their unborn child, continue visitations with one or both, was anathema to sound adoption practice.

Change has come slowly but steadily in the adoption field. Seventy years ago, the "orphan trains" were one solution as they transported thousands of homeless older youngsters to the midwest. These children were literally "put up for adoption" to any person or family who wanted them, regardless of the motivation for adoption. In the 1920s and 1930s for younger babies the agencies developed the notion of the "blue ribbon baby," reflecting the influence of the era's prevailing social Darwinist philosophy. This thinking was consonant with delayed placement to make sure that the child was free of intellectual or other deficits. When it was found that such delay created problems for both child and adoptive parents, the practice was virtually eliminated, though not overnight. (Social workers don't change *that* quickly.)

The decade of the 1960s, known for rapid social change, brought further shifts in adoptive practices. In all of these, the emphasis shifted from meeting the needs of adoptive parents to those of children of mixed racial parentage, black children, older children and sibling groups, children with physical and/or behavioral difficulties, and even children who had been emotionally damaged by their biological caretakers. Adoption, during this era, became a viable option for this group of children as well as newborn, healthy in-racial children.

These nontraditional adoptions often took the form of single-parent adoption, adoption across racial lines, and adoption by older couples. The 1970s were a time of great ferment and reversed some of the practices of the 1960s. Transracial adoption was virtually eliminated as a result of a firm stance taken by the National Association of Black Social Workers against such placements. In 1973 the Supreme Court ruled abortion legal. During the same decade the rights of birth fathers emerged as an important issue in *Stanley v. Illinois*, a Supreme Court ruling that virtually revolutionized adoption practice by extending new custody rights to fathers of illegitimate children.

While these issues became and still are controversial in their own right, the disputes they caused paled compared to the practice of "open adoption," a practice that became more common in the late 1970s. While there are many forms of open adoption, basically it represents a departure from confidentiality that characterized traditional adoptions. It ranges from a one-time meeting between adoptive parents, birth parents, and child, to regular visitation by the birth family, including extended family.

Definitional problems arise here. What represents openness in adoption to one person may not to another. For instance, would a one-time phone contact between the birth mother and prospective adoptive mother, with no exchange of identifying information, constitute an open adoption? I favor the operational definition of the continuum provided by McRoy of the University of Texas:

1. Confidential—minimal exchange of biographical/personal information on adoptive and birth parents at placement *and* either no contact between the parties after placement *or* the exchange of nonidentifying information the first year (one or two pictures, a letter update provided for the birth parents).
2. Semiopen (continued, nonidentifying)—active sharing of nonidentifying information (letters, pictures, gifts) mediated by the agency. Includes face-to-face meetings as long as parties share only nonidentifying information.

3. Full disclosure—sharing of identifying information (last names, addresses, phone numbers) *and* direct communications between parties. Often includes ongoing face-to-face contact. (personal communication 1993)

The unfortunate thing about this controversy, and it is indeed a controversy, is that advocates and critics of openness in adoption take adversarial positions. I use this term synonymously with *open* adoption. The problem is that both the critics of the practice and its defenders posture themselves mainly from anecdotal evidence (Gross 1993), producing only a state of perpetual confusion. It is my hope in this chapter to present the arguments (a term used advisedly) from both sides. An additional chapter will look at the research to date, but the reader should be aware that research in this area, particularly concerning the children, is in an embryonic stage. Indeed, we will be well into the twenty-first century before we have enough longitudinal studies to yield a realistic and reliable pattern as to the effects of the practice.

In actuality, open adoption has been practiced for years. Although always controversial, its controversy has centered around the placement of newborn infants. No one questions its use for a child placed at the time he/she is a toddler or older. But the controversy surfaces for an infant who has never experienced an extrauterine bond with his birth mother.

There is one point on which the adversaries concur. No matter how open the arrangement, the birth parents legally relinquish all parental claims and rights to the child. The adoptive parents are the child's legal parents, and the birth parents are viewed as important members of the child's extended family system who are not be involved in the day-to-day parenting (Reitz and Watson 1992). How this arrangement plays out, psychologically, from one family to the next, can vary tremendously.

Before examining the arguments pro and con, it might be well to view the contemporary practice in a historical context. For years, the subject of adoption proceedings were immersed of shame, stigma, and secrecy. Beginning in the 1940s, social workers worked with legislators to pass laws requiring the sealing of adoption records. This marked the end of a relationship (with bio-parents) and a beginning of another relationship (with adoptive parents). But this symbolic transfer did more than that. It effectively prevented birth parents and adoptees from learning about each other. Thus, for decades, social work practice in adoption stressed secrecy, anonymity, and confidentiality to protect birth mother, adoptees, and adoptive parents against the stigmas of unmarried motherhood and illegitimacy. This was not, however, an effort to "kill off" the birth parents; in fact, social workers were to be intermediaries, to pass along important but nonidentifying, information between the various parties to continue the genetic lineage that had become compromised through the adoption.

By the 1970s, society had become more accepting of female-headed households, perhaps spurred by the women's movement. Tracing one's roots and ethnic heritage gained popularity. The knowledge explosion in the behavioral sciences all but obliterated the nurture bias that social scientists had perpetuated, and replaced it with hard evidence that behavioral and personality problems were also linked to genetics. Some adult adoptees became vocal about the hurt and anger they felt about being denied access to information about their genetic antecedents. Many felt they had the right to know as much as did the agency about their own pasts. Birth parents emerged from their shadow of shame, asserting that they did not forget the children they had placed for adoption and always wondered if those children were alive, well, or even knew they were adopted. Some felt that the secrecy that surrounded the adoption made grieving their loss more complex and difficult. Some adoptive parents also began to express their frustration and feelings of helplessness over their inability to help their children connect with their biological heritage (Chapman et al. 1986; Gritter 1989).

Another issue helped spawn this new practice, which has to do with the ways agencies operate and relates to the issue of *control*. A year ago, this writer addressed a professional group on the status of adoption practice. Part of that address consisted of the following:

> Adoption today is in a state of crisis. The reason it is in a state of crisis is because we, the professionals directing its practice, have lost control. Due to the many changes affecting practice, the locus of power has shifted from the agency to the birth mother.
>
> There was a time when we were in control. Those were the days when a birth mother would walk in the door of an agency, and state, "I'm pregnant, unmarried, and I would like you to place my baby for adoption. Put him, if you will, in a nice home where a mother and father will love him and nurture him as he deserves, because I can't." The agency would agree to place the child and the expectant mother trusted in the agency judgment about the best parents, depending on the criteria set up by the birth mother (e.g. she could waive the religious matching policy). But it was the agency which made the choice. In those days, we didn't have to worry about the birth father as he was deemed to have no rights, even if he knew of the pregnancy, which in many cases, he did not. Neither did we worry about the birth mother changing her mind post placement as single motherhood was not yet acceptable. The point is that the professional, via the agency, had control over the situation. As long as this was the case, the field was in a non-crisis situation because it could look at the various principals in the triad, and evaluate the situation in this way. The child is getting a loving home, the adoptive parents can rear a child they otherwise could not have, and the birth mother, once she came to terms with the impact of her momentous decision, could go on with her life. Nice and simple, all I's dotted and T's crossed. But this scenario came to a gradual halt with the realization (by birth mothers collectively) that the agencies needed them, rather than birth mothers needing the agencies (Smith 1995).

Arguments for Open Adoption

All sides of the triad present arguments in favor of open adoption. Those who advocate open adoption contend that knowledge of one's genetic history constitutes an innate human need. They believe that denial of such knowledge prevents the development of the child's own personal identity. They argue that open adoption provides the child with a greater sense of biological connections, a deeper sense of continuity of the biological line, and a more realistic picture of his or her background and present situation.

The proponents of openness point out that (1) the secrecy that formerly mired the adoption process and that gave rise to adoptees' anxiety, is virtually eliminated; (2) birth parents feel a great deal of security and control over knowing who is rearing the child; (3) there is a ready-made opportunity to provide an ongoing account of the medical and psychiatric history of the birth family with time (Baran and Pannor 1984).

Author Jeanne Lindsay takes the position that open adoption lessens the pain for all parties in the adoption triad. She asserts that openness in adoption is the ideal form of adoption practice. She states, further, that the contacts between adoptive parents and birth parents can be made outside the realm of the agency or social worker (1987).

In response to the argument that open adoption represents the potential for loss of the child by the adoptive parents, critics of confidential adoption point to the very opposite: a lessening of the sense of loss. They point out that what stirs up fears and anxieties is not fear of the sense of loss of the child but rather the fear of the loss of the relationship between the adoptive parents and the child. The argument concludes that adoptees under an open arrangement feel a greater sense of entitlement than their confidential counterparts.

Proponents of open adoption offer other arguments. They cite as advantages that, with open adoption, adoptive parents need not fear "running into" birth parents—they can see them. Another statement heard is that adopted children don't have to fantasize about their birth parents—they can see them and have an ongoing relationship with them. In addition, open adoption provides the birth parents with a higher level of comfort over the decision to place and may even affect their decision. They can find out how the child is doing simply by making a telephone call.

Arguments against Open Adoption

The arguments against open adoption also are presented from all three sides of the adoption triangle. From the standpoint of the adoptive parents, the argument is that open adoption interferes with the parental bond so crucial to proper personality development. The psychological task of parental entitlement, a sense that the child is rightfully theirs, may be compromised in open adoption practices. To do an effective job, adoptive parents must feel that this is their own child, that they are not merely filling in for the "real" parents. The question is, "Can they do this with a perception that the birth parents may be looking over their shoulders?" Another concern for the birth parents in that, through open adoption, they do not allow themselves to grieve the loss of the child and go on with their own lives (Kraft et al. 1985). A recent study found that birth mothers under an open adoption arrangement experienced a more complicated grieving process than birth mothers who placed the child under a confidential arrangement (Blanton and Deschner 1990). However, the greatest concern about open adoption relates to the children over the passage of time.

Literature on child development suggests that the real problem (with open adoption practice) will occur during adolescence, a time when a child must work out issues of personal identity. While some data suggest that adopted adolescents are essentially no different than their nonadopted counterparts, a 1985 study by Stein and Hoopes found that people remain concerned about how most adoptees will fare under an open adoption arrangement.

A final argument against open adoption relates to the track record of confidential adoptions for over half a century. Collectively, research studies indicate that 84 percent of adoptive placements are successful, that most adoptees are not interested in meeting with their birth families, and that those adoptees who are not interested in searching have a more positive self-image than those who are interested in searching (Kadushin and Martin 1988; Aumend and Barrett 1984).

Questioning the Open Adoption Rationale

In the light of these arguments against open adoptions and because for the most part, traditional and confidential adoption has been a successful venture, how did open adoption practice get started? A number of reasons are offered. First, some clinicians became concerned when they observed that a disproportionate number of adolescents with perceptual and behavioral disturbances had been adopted, and these youngsters had questions about their origins that could not be answered given the cloak of secrecy and the sealing of birth records. Questions like "who am I really, who do I look like, from whom did I get this artistic ability" were common. The term "genealogical bewilderment" began to surface in the minds of these clinicians, and they concluded that most, if not all, adopted children were equally bothered by these questions. Second, the changing societal attitude that approved of birth mothers parenting their children brought with it a shifting of power arrangements. These birth mothers realized that they had some control over the terms under which they would place their children for adoption. A third reason is related to changes in our family structure and changes in previously stereotyped roles in family living. The women's movement has altered family structure in such a way that there are now many variations: single parenting, coparenting, blended families, and cohabiting unmarried opposite-sexed adults.

Regarding the frequently expressed relationship between emotional disturbance and adoptive status, it is fairly clear that clinicians and researcher do not look at the same phenomena the same way, but see things through different lenses. In a study of over 5,000 psychiatric patients in California, Brinich and Brinich found no significant differences between adopted and nonadopted patients. They concluded that "our data suggest that human adaptive capacities are such that the majority of adoptions can justly be characterized as successes; certainly those authors. . .who have emphasized the association between adoption and psychopathology will find little in our data to support their view (1982)."

Although a statistical relationship does exist between adoption and emotional disturbance, the relationship may be viewed as spurious in nature. Had clinicians looked further, they might have found (in the adoptive families) other explanations for the disturbance—poor communication, family violence, or alcoholism. In other words, the disturbance is not created by the adoptive status but by confounding clinical circumstances. At the same time, seeking therapy can be a positive step. Talking about feelings about being adopted can help adoptees achieve a sense of security and content. This is a misunderstanding about therapy. The problem is that when broad generalizations about a whole class of people (in this case, adoptees) are made based on the findings of a clinic population, one has sown the seeds of a theory based largely on partial truths. The tendency to draw these conclusions obliterates the most basic of research principles: research is done to generalize to a larger group—people like these—and findings cannot be extended to other, different groups. The fact is an extremely high percentage of adoptees never need to avail themselves of mental health services.

The Views of Experts

Between 1 August and 25 September 1991, this writer personally contacted a number of people eminently qualified to serve in the role of experts. Most of these people had university connections, some currently and some on emeritus status.

David Brodzinsky, a noted adoption researcher at Rutgers University, takes somewhat of a middle-of-the-road position that tends toward greater openness. While he recognized some drawbacks to open adoption, he feels it is a worthwhile option. "It is naive," he stated, "to assume that one form of adoption placement agreement will work for each child and for each family. The task of the field is to try to maximize options for all types of placements."

Lela Costin, professor emeritus at the University of Illinois, takes a similar position. She feels that the practice of open adoption is a positive move toward sound placement practice. However, she does qualify her position by stating that it should be done only in situations in which there is a clear advantage to the child, that because each case situation is unique what works for one family might be disastrous for another.

Hilda Arndt, professor emeritus at Louisiana State University, takes a cautious position insofar as the practice of open adoption is concerned. She contends that the practice should be limited to those cases in which the child has a need for meeting with the birth parent(s). If the child's questions cannot be answered through the nonidentifying information available to him/her, there should be a good deal of preparation for possible emotional reactions to such a meeting. She went on to state that the birth parents, as well, would need equal emotional preparation to deal with the child's sense of divided loyalty and identification with the adoptive parents. But it should be done on a case-by-case basis, when it is clearly a response to the child's need to solidify personal identity issues, and not as a blanket policy from birth on. Finally, she raised questions about the adolescent adoptee whose abilities to divide and conquer, setting one parent against the other, are at an all-time high.

Alfred Kadushin, a professor emeritus at the University of Wisconsin, author of many texts on child welfare practices and one who has conducted a vast amount of research on adoptions, believes that "The real problem of open adoption, despite its increasing popularity, is that children ultimately have to resolve identity issues of who they really are and loyalties to each set. If their essential identification is with their birth families and not their adoptive families, a situation is created of a high likelihood for conflict and behavioral difficulties, the result being a disruption of family living."

Beulah Compton, a professor emeritus at the University of Southern Mississippi and author of a number of textbooks on social work practice, also expressed concerns about the development of the child's identity, particularly when there are multiple parent figures. This concern is further heightened by the specter of the child sensing a disparity between the adoptive and birth parents' standard of living. If the lifestyle of the adoptive family is one of success and affluence, and the lifestyle of the birth family is one of low middle class or poverty level, the child may experience considerable difficulty in integrating the two into his/her personality and be left in a state of confusion.

Where Do We Go from Here?

Open adoption has truly revolutionized the adoption field. While confidentiality in adoption practice has worked so well for so many years, agencies are experimenting with various forms of openness because of pressure from adoptees and birth parent groups.

While the practice is highly controversial, and emotions ride high, both agree on at least one point. It is the adoptive parents who must be the child's psychological parents. Whether birth parents can assume the role of bystander while the adoptive parents rear the children in ways that are not consonant with their own ways of child rearing, only time will tell. Even those who advocate open adoption as the best form of adoption practice have their misgivings. Annette Baran and Reuben Pannor are two outspoken social workers favoring open adoption. Yet they state: "Certainly open adoptions will encounter difficulties in the same way that complicated family relationships do. Some of these relationships may be so enmeshed or difficult that the people involved sever the connections. . . . Some birth parents may be too needy. . . . Some adoptees may want too much and they may feel rejected when the response is minimal" (Baran and Pannor 1990, 331).

In the process of finding the best solution for each child, one must distinguish between the adoptee's search for more information about origins and a search for the birth family. Many adoptees wish only information, not contact. Research is needed on the percentage of adoptees who are searching and whether these contacts are helpful, traumatic, or somewhere in between.

Those conducting the research must realize that no one knows, at present, how adolescent adoptees will view the open adoption arrangement. It may not be wise to assume that they will not develop strong feelings of loyalty or guilt toward the people who brought them into the world. In some cases, they may be grateful that the open adoption option was exercised. In others, there may be considerable anger and hurt feelings. It is the lot of the researcher to determine under what circumstances open adoption is preferable, when should it be utilized, and when should it be avoided at all costs. Research efforts in the future will hopefully provide some answers to inform the practitioners what sort of policy or policies should be implemented in order to best meet the standard of what is in the best interest of the child.

I would like to add a personal note, a postscript, on this subject. As stated in chapter 2, I have altered my own view of this change in policy and practice. In my previous work (Smith and Miroff 1987), I was critical of the openness movement. I raised all sorts of questions about how the children would deal with this change in their lives. Can they separate these different parent figures and not be confused about different roles? Research has yet to answer this question, developmentally and longitudinally. At the same time, one should recognize that many adoptees have been struggling with confusing feelings about their parentage and lineage under the traditional, confidential placement system. Therefore, we should be willing to examine various other approaches, including degrees of openness.

I have always prided myself on being a realist, and one realistic feature of this entire scenario is that adoption will never be the tidy package we once thought it to be. And, like it or not, openness in adoption, including visitation, is grounded in realism.

In a subsequent chapter, I will review the research on this subject to date, as well other adoption-related empirical findings. But first, I plan to review ways to evaluate research, including revising some material from my previous book.

Chapter 6

Research in Adoption

Truth is an elusive phenomenon. Everyone claims to have a handle on it, but when it really comes down to it, the truth they believe is no more than a perception (of the truth) at best, a myth, or an outright lie, at worst. Statistics can be manipulated to support whatever one wishes to confirm or to prove.

That is the way it is in adoption practice. Much of the so-called "theory" in practice comes to us from clinical impressions of practitioners, based on a clinical sample of people with psychosocial or psychiatric disorders (who coincidentally happen to be adopted). The theory that concludes that adopted children ipso facto are emotionally disturbed has not been tested in an empirical sense. It has, nevertheless, survived over the years as if it were truth.

The status of adoption theory is so comprised. Many theoretical positions state that *their* way best explains how to make adoptions work for *everybody,* seemingly an impossible task. In essence, everybody is courting what he/she considers to be the truth. But the (presumed) truth is that one form of adoption practice might work well for family A (for a variety of perhaps idiosyncratic reasons) but another form works best for family B (perhaps for different reasons). It is the lot of the researcher to uncover and discover what those variables are that lead to personal and family satisfaction.

One illustration of this phenomenon that clearly comes to mind is the "matching" principle in adoption. The idea underlying matching was to attempt to imitate nature as well as possible. Agencies have attempted, and still do to a considerable extent, to match the child with his prospective parents, not only physically but in terms of educational values, standards, and expectations. This makes perfectly good sense on the face of it, and the practice became an inviolable procedure of sound adoption practices. However, research findings on adoption outcome and matching reveals no relationship whatsoever. In other words, those placements that attempted to match child and parents turned out to be no different that those in which matching was not used (Ripple 1968).

Another example relates to sealed records which were based on a privacy theory, on the view, right or wrong, that the sealing of the records symbolized a new beginning for the adoptive family—that all parties in the adoption triangle, including the birth mother, would be best off in the long run. Then, many parties began claiming that this practice was not in the best interest of the child. They claimed that they had empirical findings to confirm their view. They used the argument that many adoptees search for their birth parents to put to rest confused and ambiguous feelings about their personal identities. However, the reader should note that much of the so-called knowledge about the general characteristics of adoptees contain a serious methodological flaw leading to flawed conclusions of practitioners. They tried to draw conclusions based on the findings of a group of emotionally disturbed people who happened to be adopted and generalize these findings to all adoptees. The most basic of all research principles is that you can only generalize the findings to a population like this one. The same error would be made if we hand-picked the most intelligent, well-adjusted, successful people in the world, found out which ones were adopted, administered a well-known standardized personality inventory, and then paraded the results as generalizable to all adoptees.

Ideally, the way to conduct research on adoptive subjects (using people from all three sides of the triangle) is to have a pool from which one can select randomly. For example, if a researcher had a pool of 100 birth mothers selected at random from a large heterogeneous group of birth mothers, s/he could generalize the findings to other birth mothers. This is because, in the random selection process, all important variables are considered randomly distributed, and people with certain characteristics would be counterbalanced in the long run by the selection of others with the opposite set of characteristics. We know that this occurs when random procedures are used with a large enough sample. But it is neither practical nor realistic to attempt to select such a sample since these people, birth mothers, in particular, have been guaranteed privacy and anonymity for the rest of their lives. This guarantee of anonymity may be true to a lesser extent with the other two groups but the principle of privacy still holds. What we see, then, are research findings on adoption from biased samples; that is, people who volunteer to be research subjects. This procedure does not invalidate the findings, but it does limit interpretation of the data.

Because of these methodological difficulties, there have only been few systematic efforts to examine the impact of adoption itself or current adoption practices upon the development of the child. It is a difficult process for the researcher to isolate the factor of adoptive status from all other factors affecting a child's adjustment.

Thus, the interrelated variables and limitations in the sample itself present formidable problems in ferreting out the myriad factors associated with success or failure in adoption. They pose problems in interpretation of the available data. They also present formidable obstacles in obtaining answers to questions of interest to those in the adoption field. As in all research of psychosocial situations, he must convince himself (and others) that what he thinks is responsible for the occurrence of the phenomenon is truly responsible and not something else.

There has been considerable speculation that the adoptive child is more prone to develop psychiatric problems. The evidence supporting this alleged vulnerability is that adoptees are disproportionately represented in caseloads of mental health practitioners. But this argument is disputed by those who point out certain methodological flaws. Madison, for example, rejected the claim on this basis:

> In making comparisons with nonadopted children, the wrong population base is used: no allowance is made for race or urban residence, although it is well-known that clinics are largely situated in cities in certain parts of the country; no heed is paid to the economic status, although the adoptive parents described obviously had money enough (which is not always the case) to obtain psychiatric help. That adoptive parents might have less hesitance about seeking psychiatric help than natural parents is not taken into account. (Madison 1966, 257)

Another researcher points to the limitations that are accruable when the cohort under investigation cannot be considered representative and lack control groups (Brodzinsky 1993).

There may be some value in elaborating some of the methodological problems or flaws cited by Madison and Brodzinsky which frequently are overlooked in the interpretation of findings, not the least of which is the fact that certain coincidental sociocultural differences between adopted and non-adopted families were overlooked.

1. The problem of self-selection is a limiting factor in properly evaluating research results. The problem of self-selection is that when people are drawn into a sample because they possess a particular characteristic of which the investigator is unaware (in this case, adoptive status), there is a lack of control of other factors which may be intruding into the particular phenomenon under the investigation.

2. Adoptive families tend to be well-educated, upper-middle-class and success-oriented. Having sought out an agency (or other professionals) to obtain a child, they are more likely to seek the services of professionals whenever the situation calls for it.

3. Different studies vary in the degree of methodological precision, the phenomenon measured, the criteria for evaluating adoptive outcome, and the statistics employed. Among the list of outcome measures are parental satisfaction, parental ratings of the child's interpersonal adjustment, ratings of the adoptive relative to his relationship with his (adoptive) parents, academic performance of the child, and the quality of the parent-child relationship.

4. There is the problem of social desirability effects in which people respond to questions in ways they believe are the most pro-social. If they say one thing and really feel another, they are confounding the results.

5. The well-known "Hawthorne effect," named after the famous experiment at the Hawthorne Electric Company, is a factor that can limit the validity of findings. It was discovered that subjects can respond differently simply by knowing, and valuing, their participation in a human experiment.

Sampling Theory

Research is conducted using samples about which there are a great deal of misunderstanding. Many people believe that one needs a large sample to yield valid findings. This is not necessarily true. The key issue in sampling is to find a sample that is *representative* of the group to which one is generalizing. Even a large sample may not be considered representative. This is where random procedures come into play. When random procedures are used, we can consider the sample representative of the larger group. This is particularly true when the sample size is large, as one may draw a "bad sample" when the numbers are small, notwithstanding the random nature of the selection process. But when non-random procedures in selecting our subjects (e.g. a convenience sample or a quota sample), we cannot consider it to be representative even if it is representative. The ideal situation, therefore, would be to select a large sample using random procedures.

In evaluating research findings, one should be clear about the nature of the sample. Many samples are based on convenience or availability. Those who volunteer to become subjects frequently possess characteristics that nonvolunteers do not, thereby threatening the generalizability (external validity) of the findings. Volunteers tend to be better educated, from a higher social class, more sociable, and in greater need of social approval than their (nonvolunteer) counterparts (Allen 1995). Some research seems to show that volunteers are more unconventional, altruistic, self-disclosing, maladjusted, and nonconforming than nonvolunteers (Rosenthal and Rosnow 1991).

Use of Probability Theory

Sampling necessarily ties into our ability to properly evaluate our findings. The concept of "probability" is useful in deciding whether one's sample findings are meaningful enough to lead one to the conclusion that the two variables in question are related. In other words, we are concerned with the level of probability that an observed finding would occur if, in truth, there really was no relationship between the two variables under study (technically called the null hypothesis). Its value, which ranges from .01 to .99, tells us how many chances out of 100 a particular finding would have occurred by chance. Thus, the designation "p=.05" means that such a finding would occur by chance 5 times in 100 if there really is no relationship. In other words, the stronger the relationship, the smaller the probability (p). To summarize, the term "probability" has a specific meaning in evaluating outcome findings. If one adopts a decision level of .05 (which has been the conventional level of significance), then one will consider any relationship with a higher p (.10 or .15, for example) as accounted for by chance and therefore not real. Any differences with probability of .05 or less (.03, .01, for example) would be considered too large to be accounted for by chance and are therefore considered "real."

At the same time, one should be aware of the difference between statistical significance and substantive significance. Statistical significance means that one can reject the assumption of no difference. But the difference may not be of any substantive or meaningful quality and therefore not be useful.

It has been reported that a disproportionate number of adoptees are seen in psychiatric clinics, but controversy remains over whether there are psychological conflicts specific to the adoption situation. Adopted children do somehow need to face and resolve complex identity issues and this has been reported in the literature (Schechter 1964; Sorosky, Baran, and Pannor 1975). However, Kadushin, a nationally recognized child-welfare researcher, noted that a vast majority of adopted children have never been referred for psychiatric treatment (1988). Further, those cases selected on a random basis, or through a matching procedure (to ensure comparability of groups), suggest few differences, if any, between adopted and nonadopted populations. It would appear that on the face of it, adoptees are seen with greater frequency than one would expect. On the other hand, a number of studies that use larger samples and accepted scientific procedures demonstrate that, with few exceptions, adopted children develop as physically and emotionally stable as their nonadoptive peers. One might entertain the idea that differences in the methodology result in differences in outcome.

Nevertheless, certain findings have contributed significantly to our understanding of adoption, and it might be helpful to examine more closely the differences between families who do require professional help and those who do not. For those who do receive services related to adoption, there are a variety of reasons.

1. Problems of unresolved feelings about infertility (for example, "I still can't help feeling resentful whenever I see a pregnant woman.")

2. Problems revolving around entitlement (for example, "I keep asking myself if I have a right to him.")

3. Problems of the parents' disappointment over growth and development issues.

4. Problems developing from the child using adoption as a weapon in dealing with conflicts with parents.

These difficulties may play themselves out in the parent-child relationship with the result that the parents are viewed as overprotective and overdefensive in regard to handling the child.

For another group their difficulties are not related to adoption but, because the child is adopted, it is easy for the nonresearch-oriented clinician to blame the difficulty on the adoptive status. In this category fall the myriad situations in which communication among family members is contradictory, dishonest, and/or destructive. Parents who use their children as pawns for fighting with each other invariably produce a situation in which the children become troubled and therefore come to the attention of those in the mental health field. This group might also include family situations in which parents feel guilty (for whatever reason or constellation of reasons) in their day-to-day contacts with the child; the child perceives the guilt and works it to his/her advantage. It would seem, then, that the greater incidence of emotional disturbance is not related to the adoption per se, but to consequent difficulties in the parent-child relationship.

Until now, I have been referring to main effects; that is, the effect of one variable on another, such as how feelings of rejection affect behavior. But in many cases, we look at the cumulative effects as well (termed interactive effects). Thus, we might want to examine how the child's genetic predisposition to acting out interacts with poor parenting, which leads to behavioral problems.

Having cautioned the reader against drawing hasty conclusions based on the interpretations of existing findings, I will next examine some studies that may be of interest to adoptive parents. In a study at a large midwestern high school, Sandra Smith compared a group of adoptees with a group of nonadoptees, matching them on sex, age, and religious affiliation. She found that both groups favored opening the records, but that the nonadoptees were more interested in opening the sealed records than were the adoptees (p=.15). Further, she found the adoptees expressing a greater sense of obligation to their parents than their nonadoptive counterparts (p=.07).

A number of studies are universally cited in any treatise on the subject of adoption research. One such study is by Triseliotis, a social worker in Scotland, who interviewed seventy Scottish adoptees who had contacted the appropriate searching agency in Edinburgh, seeking information about their background and origins. In a second study, Sorosky et al. reported on interviews with about fifty adult adoptees who had completed reunions with their biological parents.

A detailed review of the Scottish study revealed that the adoptive parents, as a whole, violated the prescribed standard of adoption practice regarding telling. Nearly two-thirds of the children first learned about the adoption when they were eleven years of age or older, and when they did find out, the source was likely to be someone other than the adoptive parents. Age of learning about adoption was associated with satisfaction in their relationship with their parents, with younger children expressing the greatest satisfaction and the older children the least satisfaction. Those over ten years of age perceived the revelation of adoption as a shock, requiring a new orientation of the self, concomitant with the intense anger at their adoptive parents. The reader should realize, however, that this was a biased sample and not one from which to draw generalizations to all adoptees. In spite of this shortcoming, the research points out the importance of many of the points made earlier about how adoptees should be told, the age of telling, and by whom they should be told.

In many respects, Triseliotis's findings were mirrored by those of Sorosky, Baran, and Pannor although both, again, relied on self-selected subjects. They studied meetings between adoptees and birth parents that resulted from contacts solicited through newspaper accounts of their interest. They, too, did not learn that they were adopted until later in life, and learned about the adoption from someone other than their parents in one-third of the cases. Most of them, as in the Triseliotis study, saw the meeting with their birth parents as advantageous. Most reported a sense of closure and completeness in regard to identity issues. Most saw the meeting as beneficial, and none viewed it as an attempt to replace their adoptive parents. Rather, they reported, as a result of the meeting, a deeper sense of love for their adoptive parents, whom they viewed as their "psychological parents."

In both of these studies, females were found more likely search for birth parents than were males. It is interesting to speculate why. It may be that women, as future childbearers, are more sensitive to the issue of discontinuity of the biological line. Another explanation may be that, in our society, women are encouraged to express their true feelings about identity concerns. It is not that men do not share such concerns, but their overt expression may be less acceptable than for women. Still a third explanation focuses on the observation that females are taught to be more oriented toward relationships. They are more apt to try to reconnect relationships that they perceive as broken. Women turn to each other more often to mend perceived hurts. (I am indebted to Dr. Noreen Keenan for this observation.)

In a recent study (Kowal and Schilling 1985), 110 adult adoptees contacted their placement agency or a search group between 1982 and 1983. Although a nonrepresentative (of all adoptees) group, their findings showed some similarities and some differences from the previous two studies cited. In this study, one-fourth reported that they were given very little information about their own genetic background by the agency. An additional 6 percent added marginal comments indicative of their dissatisfaction with information given or that it had subsequently proved to be untrue.

This parallels the Triseliotis and Sorosky et al., studies on background information. Nevertheless, 60 percent of the subjects reported that they had been told of the adoption at an early age, according to the prescribed standard for early telling. An additional 29 percent reported not being told until their elementary school years. This would seem to indicate some salient differences between this study and the previous two studies.

One of the most interesting questions addressed in various studies relates to the feelings of adoptees about being adopted. Books written for adoptive parents have almost universally advised the appropriateness of the word "chosen" or "special" in the telling (for example, see Raymond 1955). However, Kirk (1964) takes the position that adoption carries with it some degree of "role handicap." (I prefer the term "role ambiguity" to "role handicap" as the latter suggests a rather serious limitation in carrying out the parental role. The difference may be semantic, however, or owing to our different disciplines; Kirk is a sociologist and I am a social worker.) But whichever term you favor, the emphasis on chosenness, Kirk claims, is an attempt to cover up the feelings of being disadvantaged. In the study, 35 percent reported feeling chosen or special; 22 percent reported feeling no different from anyone else; 25 percent reported being worried about it; and 17 percent reported feelings of embarrassment. Thus, there was a range of attitudes, and it is perhaps most interesting that 57 percent of the adoptees felt reasonably positive about adoption. (Remember, this sample of adoptees contacted the agencies responsible for their placement.)

Much has been written about identity conflicts of adolescent adoptees and many of the theoretical concerns are identified later (see chapter 9). Sorosky and his colleagues believed that their findings support their belief that adoptees are more vulnerable than the general population to identity conflicts in late adolescence and early adulthood.

In the largest, most comprehensive study on adoption outcome, Benson and his colleagues amassed data through a random sample of 715 families, looking at issues of identity, mental health, attachment, and family stability (Benson, Sharma, and Roehlkepartain 1994). Using data on children adopted during infancy, obtained through both public and private agencies in four states, they found the following:

1. Adopted adolescents scored as well as their nonadopted siblings relative to identity issues.

2. A strong emotional attachment was found to exist between the adoptee and his/her adoptive parents.

3. Parents' openness to discussing adoption was positively related to adoptive adjustment while parental difficulty in accepting differences between themselves and the children was negatively associated with sound mental health functioning.

4. Most adoptees reflect a positive view in regard to their adoptive status.

While this study, important and far-reaching as it was, significantly contributed to our knowledge base on adoption outcome, it was nevertheless limited: (1) there was no control group (of nonadopted families); (2) there was a sizable number of families (40 percent) who declined participation; and (3) there was a group, though small, of nonrespondents—families who initially agreed to participate, yet did not (8 percent).

This finding parallels an interesting study of identity crises of both adoptees and nonadoptees, as reported by Norvell and Guy (1977). In comparing self-concept scores between the two groups, they found no significant differences, and concluded that "adoptive status itself cannot produce a negative identity. If negative elements become incorporated in the adolescent's identity, they more likely than not stem from problems within the home" (p. 445).

Other research efforts have yielded similar results. In a recent comparison between searchers and nonsearchers (looking for critical differences between the two groups), the nonsearchers had a more positive self-image than did the searchers (Aumend and Barrett 1984).

Loper (1976) was interested in comparing searchers and nonsearchers, not on the basis of identity issues but on key personality factors and social variables. Breaking her sample down to three separate groups (from those with no interest in their biological parents to those with an active interest), she concluded the following:

1. Nonsearchers had more positive self-concepts than searchers ($p=.01$);

2. Nonsearchers had more positive attitudes toward their adoptive parents. They viewed their adoptive parents as more emotionally involved in a positive way than did searchers;

3. Although the nonsearchers learned of their adoption at earlier ages than their counterpart searchers, the difference was not statistically significant;

4. Concerning a rating of "overall happiness," a disproportionate number of nonsearchers reported a "very happy" or "mostly happy" life (90 percent) compared with searchers (41 percent); and

5. Nonsearchers began living with their adoptive family at an earlier age than did searchers. Nearly 90 percent of the nonsearchers were placed prior to six months of age compared to 80 percent of the searchers.

Overall, the study seems to cast doubt on the alleged vulnerability of all adoptees. Based on the study findings, adoptees tend to have positive self-concepts, are reasonably satisfied with their relationships with their parents, and revealed critical differences between searchers and nonsearchers.

While there is much we do not know relative to adoption success, there is much we do know. We know that the vast majority of adoptive placements are successful, that boys are more likely than girls to develop some form of conduct disorders (whether this has anything to do with the adoption is not known), but girls are more likely to search. We know that children with a history of previous deprivations and multiple placements, especially within their first two years of life, are at a higher risk of adoption failure. We know that adoptions in which the adoptive parents have excessive expectations of the child are at a high risk.

A number of variables, previously thought to bear on outcome and therefore major issues in agency adoption practice, proved to have no factual basis. These include: background factors of the child; adoptive parents' age; length of marriage; income and educational level; socioeconomic status; and religion. As stated previously, attempts to match infants' potential with parents' characteristics and expectations proved unsuccessful. The principal factors seem to be parental attitudes toward the child—their unconditional acceptance of him and the degree to which they have worked through feelings of entitlement.

Overall, these findings suggest that adoption works well, particularly for those who are adopted in infancy and where there are already indications of family stability and strength. Yet there are other findings that suggest that adoptees are a particularly vulnerable group *and there are data to support that claim.* Brodzinsky (1990) notes this in his statement that

Adopted children are at increased risk for psychological and academic problems [which]. . . generally do not manifest themselves until the elementary school age years. Furthermore, it is clear that adopted children display a wide range of adjustment patterns, with only a minority presenting evidence of clinically significant symptomatology. Indeed, most adopted children appear to cope quite well with the challenges, conflicts, and demands of adoptive family life. (p. 23)

Finally, the reader will note that none of the findings in this chapter examine the research on openness in adoption. This is because there are a number of new and fairly recent studies, important and unique enough in its magnitude and implications to warrant their own chapters. That is what will be addressed next in this book.

Chapter 7

Research on Open Adoption

In theory, decisions in practice are guided by empirical findings that emerge from research, preferably done by investigators with a clinical background. But in many cases, practice changes are not preceded by empirical findings; rather, changes in practice inform what sort of research should be engaged in to confirm or disconfirm practice decisions already put into operation. In many cases, these changes are put into effect by ideological shifts, while in other cases, they are effected by no more than a hunch that another approach might work better.

That is the way openness in adoption has evolved, with much burgeoning research evidence developing subsequent to practice. In evaluating the research-based state of the art in adoption, Barth's statement has a ringing effect:

> The history of adoption has involved cycles of relatively narrow thinking by practitioners about what was acceptable adoption practice followed by willingness to consider broader possibilities. . . . Researchers have a responsibility to see that information continues to flow into the field to encourage more inclusive research-based understanding (1994, 626).

The field is in the process of evaluating a host of research efforts, either currently underway or completed. By far, the modal form has been cross-sectional, that is, data collected at one point in time. Most are nonprobability samples, characterized by the use of nonrandom procedures. They tend to be exploratory, descriptive, and nonrepresentative. Many of them fall under the heading of survey research and none (insofar as this author is aware) has approximated an experimental or even a quasi-experimental design. Nevertheless, what has been generated about how openness has worked is valuable in our never-ending search to find better ways of helping people build families that are functional and lead to satisfaction, if not happiness, for all family members.

Research in this area is evolving and, necessarily is tentative. Anecdotal evidence, although not statistically meaningful, is nevertheless one place to start. Kraft et al. (1985) argued that openness intensifies identity conflicts for the adoptee while Gritter (1989) and Silber and Dorner (1990) suggest the intensification of such conflicts under a confidential arrangement. Another author strongly suggests that the benefits that await a birth mother who participates in an open adoption may persuade her to relinquish her child before she is emotionally ready (Cocozelli 1989). It is not yet clear whether openness dilutes the genealogical bewilderment seen in some adolescent adoptees. Some evidence suggests, however, that knowledge about one's background and personal history contributes to a sense of identity and security (Cline 1987; Smith 1987).

Other studies, using small samples, are reported by Berry (1991). Some are from her own research and some were carried out by others (McRoy et al., 1988; Belbas 1987; Siegel 1993; Gross 1993). Collectively, some of the findings are:

1. A moderately high level of satisfaction exists on the part of both sets of parent figures;

2. Entitlement issues for the adoptive parents allegedly were not compromised through an open adoption arrangement;

3. Adoptive parents take comfort in knowing that their children will have ready access to information regarding their genetic past;

4. The McRoy study found greater satisfaction with the semiopen arrangements inasmuch as all parties seem to benefit more from this arrangement more than from the two other forms (1988);

5. Some adoptees report continued sense of grieving for the birth parents, related to their sense of loss, confirming the findings of another study (Blanton and Deschner 1990);

6. Adoptive parents reported a sense of relief that their children would be able to access birth-related information usually denied them by the sealed record system;

7. Adoptive mothers felt empathy with the birth mothers.

However, one should be aware of unanticipated negative consequences of open adoption. Siegel (1993) does a nice job in outlining some of these, which fall into the area of long-term effects on the child. As stated by one adoptive mother, "It's like climbing a mountain blind. I feel there is no roadmap."

Two Additional Studies

There are two studies that provide some contrast to each other and that I would like to present at some length. The first was carried out by Ruth McRoy and her associates at the University of Texas. Her study examined the consequences of adoption along the continuum suggested in the previous chapter. The second study was conducted by the author after consulting with Dr. McRoy. I use her continuum with her permission.

The differences between these two studies are: (1) different samples; (2) different data collection methods; and (3) different methods of analysis. McRoy's study was based on interview data of 190 adoptive fathers and mothers, with approximately one-third of the sample in each of the three groupings. Children had already been placed with these families; thus, a placement bias was in effect. My study was conducted with 70 preadoptive families whose homes had been approved by the respective agencies but had not yet received a child. Hence, I was able to avoid the placement bias. McRoy points out, however, in citing my work, that a selection bias was in effect inasmuch as the agencies I used were, at that period in their history, confidential adoption agencies (McRoy et al. 1994).

Summary of McRoy's Findings

1. An "overwhelming majority" of all adoptive parents, irrespective of level of openness, reflected satisfaction over the birth parents' involvement.

2. Those adoptive parents in the mediated and fully disclosed adoptions cited their experiences with the birth parents as wanting more or less involvement from and with them. Most who were satisfied wanted more contact and those who were dissatisfied attributed this dissatisfaction with a variety of issues, such as a unilateral decision by the birth parents' or an agency policy decision.

3. Fear of the birth parent reclaiming the child was virtually nonexistent. This was particularly true for the confidential adoptions, no doubt a function of the protection inherent in the system.

4. Perceptions of entitlement were essentially the same, that is, were not statistically significant in the three groupings. The most commonly coded rating on this item was "very secure."

In the discussion, the authors make a number of salient points: (1) openness should be viewed as an ongoing process rather than as a static state of affairs; (2) Kirk's "shared fate" theory (1964) should be expanded to include the birth family, including extended family members; (3) parents who have a clear sense of entitlement tend to feel more confident about the permanence of their children; and (4) this study was conducted using only volunteer participants, hence no one should generalize them to all adoptive families; that these findings are tentative and should be viewed that way. Ruth McRoy stated the matter thusly: "Different strokes for different folks" (personal communication 1993); and that what works best for one family may work to another family's detriment.

Smith Study

This exploratory study was conducted to determine people's views toward open adoption before they received a child in their home. After meeting with the couples personally to explain the research objectives, the couples then completed a rather lengthy self-administered questionnaire. These couples were drawn from a number of agencies in the south and midwest: Gladney Adoption Center in Fort Worth, Texas; the Cradle in Evanston, Illinois; Coleman Adoption Service, Adoption Support Center, and Adoption Services, Incorporated, all located in Indianapolis. It is this writer's understanding that Gladney and the Cradle are now operating under an openness policy.

Findings

In a descriptive statistical breakdown, several measures of central tendency revealed the following: the mean age was 33.5 years, the median 34 years, and the modal age was 35. This made the sample a virtually normal distribution. The educational level was, indeed, a normal distribution as all three measures of central tendency were 16 years of formal education or a bachelor's degree. Income, however, varied, with the mean family income being $93,000, while the median income was $70,000, and the modal income $60,000. The range of income was very wide, with the lowest family income being reported at $36,000 and the highest at $300,000.

Occupationally and professionally, this group of people represented a cross section of professionally and financially competent adults. The largest group were in the sales/management area, with 44 percent of respondents falling into that category. The following professions were also represented: medicine; nursing; law; education; dentistry; engineering; accountancy; and interior design/decorating. This survey conforms to other demographic analyses that show that adoptive parents tend to be upper-middle class, well educated, with a high level of social and professional competence.

Perceptions of Adoptive Parents (APs) in Study

Type of Placement:

A. Open (Full Disclosure)

Perceived Advantages	Perceived Disadvantages
1. Questions unanswerable by background material can be answered	1. Impairment of bonding relationship between APs and child
2. Eliminate curiosity about looks when a child does not resemble adoptive parents	2. Sense of entitlement diluted or compromised
3. Advantage to birth parents in feeling secure of soundness of placement	3. Disruptive of family life
	4. Feeling of having to share child— robs one of a sense of exclusiveness of parent-child relationship
	5. Life confusing enough to child without having to accommodate to extra set of parents, grandparents, aunts, uncles, etc.

B. Semi-Open

Perceived Advantages	Perceived Disadvantages
1. Curiosity about looks and characteristics of birth parents muted	1. Dual parental identification may be confusing
2. Can be reassuring to birth parents—give them sense of control of situation	2. Entitlement compromised to some extent
3. Child receives more realistic picture of adoptive situation	3. Loss of confidentiality
4. Reduces guilt, anguish of birth parents relative to their decision	
5. May encourage some (ambivalent birth parents around placing) to make placement plan	

C. Confidential

Perceived Advantages	Perceived Disadvantages
1. Entitlement has best working for APs and child	1. May not have much chance of background info to go on—may leave child wondering
2. Much easier to go on with own lives—for all parties concerned	2. Sharing background may be quite limited
3. No confusion as to "real parentage"	3. Changes in medical history not accessible
	4. Leaves birth parents wondering how child is faring

Finally, my findings on other agency practices are noteworthy. By providing the subjects with a range of topics, I was able to discern the intensity of agreement or disagreement via a Likert-type scale. The scores ranged from "1" to "5", "1" meaning a strong disagreement, "5" meaning strong agreement.

Statement	Mean Score
1. I am confident that the agency will place a child with us within the expected time frame discussed with us.	3.42
2. I am confident that the child placed with us will have characteristics and background that match our own.	3.47
3. I anticipate that we (my spouse and I) may need to modify our attitudes about the conditions under which the placement will be made (e.g., meeting with the birth parents).	2.44
4. I would be willing to meet with one or both of the birth parents one time prior to the placement.	3.01
5. I would feel comfortable with meeting with one or both of the birth parents.	2.58
6. I would want to meet with one or both of the birth parents whether or not the agency worker suggested it.	2.04
7 An adoptee should have the right of access to all information about his/her birth parents, including their identities.	3.04
8. Adopted children should be able to obtain sufficient background information about their genetic origins, but not actual identities of birth parents.	3.61
9. I wonder if I will be as good a mother (father) as this child deserves.	2.87
10. I think sharing of identities does not interfere with	3.07

being good adoptive parents.

11. A child should be told of his adoption by the time   4.31
    she/he is four years old.

12. Bringing a child up that one adopts is no different   2.91
    than bringing up a biological child.

13. Adopted children should be told about their   4.87
    adoption.

14. Adopted children should not be told that their   3.70
    conception was the result of a rape, if that was the
    circumstance.

15. Adopted children should be told that their   2.44
    conception was a result of incest, if that was the
    circumstance.

16. I look forward to telling my (adopted) child about   3.67
    the fact of his/her adoption.

17. I am fearful of telling my (adopted) child about the   2.32
    fact of his/her adoption.

18. I have a fearful fantasy that the day will come when   2.50
    my child's birth parents will intervene in our lives.

19. It makes me anxious to think that, after we have   2.50
    adopted, well-meaning people (relatives, neighbors)
    will ask us personal, intrusive questions about our
    child's ancestry.

20. It will bother me if my child comes to me and asks   2.35
    what the word "illegitimacy" means.

21. It is a good idea to tell my child that she/he was   4.17
    placed for adoption out of the birth parent's love for
    her/him.

Male and female attitudes did not significantly differ for most of these statements. For those that did, the following surfaced. Using the level of significance at .10:

1. Females were more likely to be willing to meet with the biological parents than males (3.2–2.8). This was significant at the .09 level. The difference may stem from the often-made observation that women have a more intense interest and curiosity over matters of reproduction and genetics.
2. Females also disagreed with men about the statement that it is not necessary to give adopted children information regarding their origins (2.03–1.46, p=.006). Women were also more emphatic regarding the need to tell a child of his/her adoption by the time he/she is four years old (4.00–4.63, p=.003). Finally, women are more bothered by the statement that people ask intrusive questions.

By far, the most significant differences were along the lines of religious preferences. The following table reveals attitudinal differences between Catholic and Protestant subjects.

Table 1

Variable	Catholic	Protestant	P Level
1. I am confident agency will place within expected time frame.	3.71	3.33	.10
2. I am confident there will be good match.	3.19	3.57	.09
3. We may need to modify our attitudes about placement conditions.	2.95	2.26	.01
4. We are willing to meet with the birth parents one time prior to placement.	3.57	2.83	.01
5. I would feel comfortable meeting with birth parents.	3.33	2.26	.001

6. I would want to meet with biological parents whether or not agency worker suggested it.	2.71	1.72	.001
7. Sharing of identities does not interfere with being good parents.	3.67	2.78	.003
8. Bringing up an adopted child is no different than a biological child.	2.62	3.04	.09
9. Adopted children should be told circumstances of their conception.	3.62	2.89	.01
Not told about rape	3.38	3.80	.10
Told about incest	2.76	2.29	.06
10. I am fearful of telling child of adoption.	2.10	2.46	.08
11. I am bothered by explaining illegitimacy.	2.10	2.48	.06

In reviewing these data, it becomes evident that a conservative element comes through to the Protestant population. On virtually every variable, they seem to be more resistant, more fearful, and less willing to recognize the place and purpose of adoption in their child's life.

Summary and Conclusions

Openness in adoption has revolutionized the practice of adoption in ways unheard of three decades ago. The change in practice has challenged the assumptions underlying the confidential form used since the early 1900s. A number of preliminary findings indicate that the practice, insofar as adoptive parents and birth parents are concerned, appears to be working reasonably well.

But the field may have paid a price for this change. On the positive side, birth parents can become an integral part of the child's life, and questions about background, family illnesses, looks, and interests can be answered. Birth parents can be viewed as a realistic presence in their children's lives and take away the fantasy of what the birth family was like. On the minus side, adoptive parents need to make room for the presence of birth parents, possibly shutting down their sense of an exclusive parent-child relationship. Viewed systemically, any change in one part of the system necessarily changes other parts. It does change the system and, as stated by Belbas (1987), "open adoption is a complicating factor emotionally."

While one is tempted to take comfort in the preponderance of success stories with confidential adoptions, it is also true that many adoptees have suffered great pain because the information they received was too limited. Will greater openness provide them with the answers to their questions in ways that will ameliorate and help resolve feelings of loss and bewilderment? We don't know.

The results of my own study should be viewed as an historical piece of work. The attitudes and perceptions of adoptive parents were elicited from the standpoint of confidentiality and before a child had been placed with them. I might be tempted to contact these same people to determine if changes in their attitudes have occurred, and in which direction. This would make for an interesting study, methodologically (individual subject variance being zero) since no one is more like yourself than yourself.

Without exception, the authors of the various studies suggest caution in evaluating the results thus far. How a child interprets the role(s) of birth families is at the center of the debate, and we owe it to the children to continue research efforts that will best inform the way practice ought to be delivered (Berry 1993). Only then will we be able to state, professionally, with whom the practice works best and worst, and under what circumstances. It is this writer's belief that the degree of openness will not, in and of itself, be the best predictor of personal stability and security in a(n) (adopted) child's life, but rather, the totality of other life circumstances, including: (1) a good gene pool; (2) degree of family openness and willingness to discuss a wide range of issues; (3) the ability of the parents to be emotionally honest and communicate honestly with each other and other family members; (4) a sound, mutually satisfying marriage; (5) entitlement issues being worked out by the parents and the child; and (6) an agreed-upon, satisfying arrangement (in the case of an open adoption) between the adoptive family and the birth family. This may seem a tall order, but it is not an impossible goal.

Chapter 8

Psychological Development of the Latency-Aged Adoptee

The latency-aged child is one who falls between the ages of seven to eleven (just prior to adolescence). The term "latency" derives from the observation that psychologically, the youngster's development is in a state of dormancy—in effect, a lull before the storm of adolescence.

Most adoptive parents are no different than biological parents in their concern over their child's psychological development. Questions surface in their minds about the best way to teach children responsibility within a value framework that stresses concern for their fellow human beings while striving to be competitive and successful. Adoptive parents share all of the concerns of their biological counterparts (in many cases, parents are both adoptive and biological parents), but adoptive parents have additional concerns related to the fact of adoption.

Some of these concerns are medical, particularly if the medical history is not complete or is vague—not being sure who the birth father is, for example, or not knowing that much about him. Some involve uncertainty of the child's intellectual endowment. All these concerns become intensified when there are gaps in the medical and personal history and are attenuated when such a history is reasonably complete. A third area of concern may arise if the parents have unresolved feelings and fears about their own right to the child. The situation is then ripe for them to project blame to the adoptive situation. Whatever the case, it is hard to evaluate the child's adjustment to life without taking into account the nature of the parents' adjustment in many areas of their own lives.

For the adopted child, this latency period is a most critical stage, perhaps *the* most critical stage. It is during this time that he comes to understand that for his adoption to have taken place, the mother who bore him had to have given him up. The perception of rejection comes as an affront to a child who had heretofore thought of himself/herself as wanted, chosen, and special. It could well come across as a crisis event, stirring up all sorts of feelings. Instead of feeling wanted or special, he/she now feels unwanted and/or undesirable. The question "why" comes up over and over again, in a multitude of ways and a variety of expressions. The wise and caring parent is able to speak to these feelings, and this interaction then turns into a feeling of being emotionally supported. Conversely, if one of the family rules (either implicit or explicit—and every family has rules) is not to express feelings, then the child has no recourse but to retreat feeling lonely, isolated, and angry.

The research of David Brodzinsky of Rutgers University on children's experience of adoption provides empirical evidence that children begin to fully understand, intellectually and emotionally, what adoption really means in their lives at approximately the age of seven or eight (Brodzinsky et al. 1984). As the child explores the world—school, peer relationships, and work—he/she understands for the first time the process involved in a woman giving birth and deciding not to raise the child but to relinquish parental responsibility to others. This can be stressful for the child who comes to terms with an absence of a biological link with his/her family.

Brodzinsky later adapted the Erikson model to suggest what goes on in the mind of an adoptee during these years of heightened vulnerability and plasticity (1990). Erikson constructed a typology of personality growth in which the individual grapples with polar development tasks. During the latency years, the nuclear conflict is that of industry (meaning the world of work via schooling) versus inferiority (Erikson 1963). Between the ages of eight and eleven, the child understands cognitively the process of giving birth and relinquishment, how this applies to him/her, and what feelings this stirs up towards all parent figures involved. This process continues during the adolescent years.

This is the beginning of a long process of dealing with *loss,* with the loss of the most meaningful relationship with the one person who is most responsible for his/her being in this world. But as the child moves on into adolescence and beyond, this sense of loss pervades every niche and cranny of his/her sense of biological connections, development, and life goals. It is not only a loss of the birth parents' identity, but of an entire family history on two sides of the aisle. Rosenberg (1992) goes so far as to state that it is a loss of normal status, that of their peers who live with their biological relatives. She states further that

> adoption signals a loss of innocence. The childlike belief that the world is fair, predictable, and trustworthy is dispelled. Instead, there develops a lifelong struggle to cope with the reality of this alternative family structure and the need

to understand why it had to be this way. (127)

I would like to add an important proviso here. That is, particularly in confidential adoptions, where the fantasy is the reality, it is absolutely necessary that the child has as complete a picture as possible of the birth parents—not just height, weight, eye and hair color, but their interests, hobbies, and the things they did especially well or poorly, because the genetic link will always be there. I say this because it has been my experience, backed up by research, that the most frustrating, even potentially rage-inducing, experience is not having any information, or very limited information, about the birth family.

I would like to stress, also, that adoptive parents are not helpless pawns in this scenario. True, they did not give birth to their children but that fact does not make them any less their children's psychological parents, a term used by Albert Solnit and his associates at Yale University (Solnit, Freud, and Goldstein 1973). But this is where adoptive parents have to look within themselves in the most critical of areas—specifically, how do they feel about themselves as this child's parent? Am I deluding myself about these feelings? Do I overreact to situations that normally do not call for such? Do I find myself saying "because I'm your parent" (the sociological authority approach) or "this is the way it is in our family, and while I respect your feelings about the situation, I trust you will respect mine" (the psychological approach). The reader will recognize these questions as bearing on entitlement issues—that one can only ascertain by inference, by a retrospective analysis of whatever actually occurred in the day-to-day interaction. (That is why I am rather dubious about research accounts that argue that entitlement issues can be determined through a pencil and paper or even an unstructured interview procedure.)

I struggle with myself having to say this, because I am an adoptive father as well, and my own children, adoptive and biological, are all overachievers, but here goes. Knowing you are adopted leads you to question your own desirability or acceptability. If you have a loving family, and you perceive it that way, you can use that knowledge as reassurance of your value. But if you don't feel your family loves you, perhaps feeling that whatever you do just isn't good enough, that perception brings with it further internal struggles. Then, as you are going through school, you find that you have other talents (artistic, musical, intellectual, physical—anything that society values), and those can reinforce your sense of self-worth. How adoptees process the information that they were given up is critical to developing a sense of peace, or being okay as a person. They all deal with loss but this should not be equated with a perception of undesirability. Also, there are opportunities to excel, and many do. The National Council for Adoption has, for years, inducted athletes into their Adoption Hall of Fame—Greg Louganis, Scott Hamilton, and Peter and Kitty Carruthers, to name a few. I suspect they will add the name of Dan O'Brien, an adoptee who won a gold medal at the 1996 Olympics for the decathlon.

I do not wish to draw undue attention to the role adoption plays in the family. It should not be overlooked, but neither should it be overstressed. It is part of the gestalt. And while it is dangerous to attribute all maladjustment to the adoptive status, it would be just as wrong to assume that the child has no feelings about it, and therefore, it may be discounted. It is a variable to be considered as part and parcel of the family constellation, and how the family deals with adoption is most critical. Consider the following case:

> Doug was a twelve-year-old who appeared at the clinic looking quite anxious. He was brought in by his parents for being disobedient at home. He sported a bruise on his face which he claimed was inflicted by his father as he was kicked downstairs. Doug went on to say that this was his own fault as he had made his father angry much of the time. In fact, he stated, "I'm used to it." He stated that his father is always "on his case" for something, particularly his grades, and has told him from time to time that he will never go far in life. Doug said that his mother yells at him a lot and predicts that he will always be in trouble and be a source of embarrassment to the family.
>
> Regarding background information, he stated that he is one of five adopted children but denied that any of his problems have anything to do with that. His main difficulty was in his attitude toward his father, who treats him unkindly. Regarding his parents, he feels he owes them a great deal but is bothered by the continued bickering between his parents. He looked quite sad as he told the therapist, "I have never seen them even touch each other."

This particular case illustrates family situations in which the adoption theme might become scapegoated. Family tension was high, and the family's adjustment was marginally adequate. Love was not fostered either between the parents or between parents and children. Doug received very few messages from his parents that would enable him to develop a positive self-image; consequently, he engaged in a host of self-deprecatory remarks consistent with the theme that he would always be in trouble. Yet it was not the adoption that brought this family in for treatment, although one could question what the agency worker was thinking about in placing so many children with such a psychologically impoverished set of parents.

In a family in which love abounds, and the parents feel good about themselves as competent human beings, the child ought to receive positive strokes or reinforcements. This will help him as he attempts to integrate the idea of being adopted into the fabric of his personality.

Family life is another important dynamic in the life of the adoptee. In fact, it is so important that it might merit a separate chapter. For now, suffice it to say that the child's personality is woven from the cloth of many interacting variables: the marital relationship, its openness and authenticity, the degree of communication and intimacy between family members, the mutuality of support of members for one another and how the family functions as a unit. The love a child is able to enjoy and express later in life depends to a certain extent on the examples provided for him in the matrix of his own family. Issues of intimacy, closeness, trust, genetics, and hopefulness provide the basis of the adult personality later on in life. This is a lesson we see manifested in countless ways, totally independent of the adoptive theme.

Perhaps the most crucial factor in the psychological development of the child rests in the process known as "identification." Children learn and take on the feelings and attitudes of their parents; that is, who or what their parents are (including, for the adopted child, his birth parents). The personality of the child is developed through identification with the parents' conscious and unconscious image of the child as one who is loved and as one who is to be trusted as he learns. Angry orders or suspicions weaken the child's self-esteem, convey a lack of trust in the child and provide him with an alternative to what he is told to do. The healthy parents, and I am including the birth parents, if the child knows them, are firmly convinced that the child will repress unacceptable impulses; the unhealthy parents do not take this attitude—in fact, they may predict undesirable behaviors. With whom the child identifies as parent figures, depends to a considerable extent on what s/he has been told about the nature of her/his relationship with this person (or people).

Almeda Jolowicz (1969) provides a case example of the effect of the "hidden parent." Paul was a boy born out of wedlock but was never relinquished for adoption. He was placed in several foster homes until he was three years old, when he settled in the one in which he grew up. Throughout the years his mother never visited, the boy never asked about her, and it is unclear whether she was even referred to, or if so, how, by the foster parents. The boy seemingly enjoyed a positive relationship with the foster parents, but when he reached adolescence, his behavior proved increasingly problematic. He refused to do his farm chores and would abruptly leave them. He let it be known that he no longer had to obey and began to ask a host of questions about his birth mother, a person he could never remember seeing. In desperation, the foster parents requested his replacement (a euphemism in the literature for being kicked out) and there followed a series of unsuccessful placements in other foster homes.

This illustration, as well as countless others, makes one ask certain questions about the effect of the fantasied parent-child bond. How could a boy who had never known his birth mother be so influenced by her that after ten years of patient and loving care by foster parents, he rejected them completely? Are his feelings of having been rejected by his birth mother so strong that he felt he had to do likewise to those who cared for him? Is there something about an original parent-child relationship that gives a parent such mysterious control over a child, even in absentia? Whence comes this power?

To answer some of these questions, we must confront a long-standing myth. That is the mistaken notion that one needs to only remove a child from a bad environment to a growth-producing one for the latter environment to negate the effects of the former. That may be the way it should work, but it doesn't. The fact is that each child does have an inner life in which he tries to hold on to the notion that his parents (meaning the people who produced him) were decent, and even honorable, people. To hear comments to the contrary is objectionable and will certainly make the child defensive. Rather than forgetting about these people, a separation may lead to the idealization of this person or these people. And in the case just cited, one very obvious factor, which necessarily complicated the picture in terms of this boy's sense of identity, was the failure of the agency to obtain a termination of parental rights so this child would be free for adoption. Whether such action would have prevented acting out behavior previously described is academic—but certainly, the foster parents in this case would have felt a greater bond with the child than they obviously felt.

This case explain why a given child will identify with adults he has never seen, but fantasized about, through the accounts of various foster parents and caseworkers.

In another example, a biologist and a former teacher adopted twelve-year-old Mary. They had met the criteria set up by the agency: Catholic, childless, mother a full-time homemaker. The adoptive plan was at the adoptive mother's wish; she was already peri-menopausal, and the likelihood of her getting pregnant was quite remote. The adoptive father asked many questions, during the preplacement investigatory period, but successfully suppressed his concerns about Mary's biological mother, who had quite a track record with men.

The adoption plan seemed to be working well, with Mary and the adoptive mother doing many things together, like shopping and going to church. But the father felt uncomfortable in Mary's presence, and with budding pubescence at the threshold, overreacted to Mary's choice of clothing and flirtatious behaviors around boys in the neighborhood. One evening, in the middle of an argument about Mary's curfew, he confronted her with his fears: that she would turn out exactly as did her (promiscuous) mother. The fact is that there was already too much of Mary's mother in her, and it did not take her long to provoke her own rejection by simply repeating old behaviors. Within a matter of days, the agency was asked to remove Mary.

Unfortunately, this is a scenario that we in the child welfare field see all too often. The fact is the more times a child is removed from a home (foster or adoptive) the greater the likelihood s/he will continue this pattern of behavior that will lead to further rejection and replacement. In many ways the child engineers this pattern, albeit unconsciously. (I believe it has to do with failure to trust other human beings, going back to Erikson's notion of the nuclear conflict during the first year of life.)

During the latency stage of development the child is attempting to work on his/her own identity. Part of this is the personal identity ("who am I, what distinguishes me from other people?") but part of this is a family identity. Values of the family come into the picture, whether through education, religious practices, or athletic achievement. The child must receive unequivocal messages about family beliefs and must observe behaviors that are consonant with those beliefs. To do otherwise is to court confusion, followed by acting-out behaviors. The adoptive parent who says, "You're mine despite the fact that someone else gave birth to you," tells the child that his "real" family is his adoptive family. If all such messages are this direct and honest, development probably takes place unimpeded. If, however, parents express their disappointment in the child's behavior and relate it to the child's heredity, he receives an unintended message that compromises his place in the family.

Parents can take measures to solidify the child's identity. Memorabilia in one form or another should be made available to him/her. A video tape provides a live re-enactment of the child's first day with the family, together with emotional reactions of all family members. Photographs taken on the day he came to the family should be placed in his growth book. (Every child should have such a book, whether adopted or not.) It becomes a part of him. There are, however, children's growth books specifically for adopted children. I do not recommend such books because I believe this draws an undue amount of attention to the fact of adoption.

Another measure that the parents may take to solidify the child's identity is through the drawing of a family tree. Family trees have become increasingly popular over the years and, in my view, are the reflection of the current emphasis on roots. Children are frequently asked to draw their own family tree which can present a dilemma for many adopted children. Knowing that another family is out there, should s/he include them—if so, is he being disloyal to his adoptive family? If he doesn't include them, is he being less than honest with himself/herself and his/her teacher? My own advice on this point has changed. I used to tell people that the child's real family tree ought to consist exclusively of the adoptive family. I no longer hold to that view, particularly in open adoption situations. I now opt for a family tree that is a microcosm of the child's sense of identity and family identification. If it involves two families, the child ought to draw two families. Realistically, she is a product of both heredity and environment, and so the family tree ought to to include both sets.

While on the subject of the family tree and school assignments, parents should be aware of teachers' comments and attitudes and those of schoolmates. Children can be cruel. As members of our society, both teachers and classmates fall prey to society's biological chauvinistic biases. For example, I recall talking to an eight-year-old girl who told me how uncomfortable she became when a schoolmate said to her, right out of the blue, "You're adopted, aren't you?"

Taken aback by this remark, she replied, "You are weird." When I asked why she responded that way, since, in fact, she was adopted, my diminutive friend said that she didn't know. It was a fear response; she didn't know what this schoolmate would do with this bit of information. "Why give her this ammunition?" An eleven-year-old told me that they were discussing adoption in class, whereupon the teacher, with all of her knowledge and authority, made the following statement: "There are three reasons why children are put up for adoption. They are either abused, unwanted, or left on a doorstep." With friends like that, who needs enemies?

The attitude of the adoptive parents toward the biological parents is critical. They cannot mask feeling threatened or competitive towards them; and these feelings will come out in discussions in one way or another. That is why the first task is to know your own feelings. Once acknowledged, you will be in a much better position to control them.

The most grievous error parents can make is to assume their child does not have feelings about being adopted. The questions "Why was I adopted?" "Was I so undesirable that a decision was made to deprive me of my birthright?" may suggest a good deal of anguish about his/her adoptive status. Such questions are painful, and there is increasing evidence that children between the age of six and adolescence continually contend with them. The realization that one was once given up, or rejected, can be a blow to the growing child's developing sense of self-worth.

It is not only beneficial but necessary to allow the child to express these feelings of hurt and rejection. Children who are allowed do so are, in the long run, emotionally healthier than children who are unable or unwilling to express their feelings. Psychodynamically, what has occurred is that the psychic energy previously tied to suppressing these emotions is now freed up to use more constructively. Once these feelings are expressed, the parent can universalize the emotion by suggesting that all adopted children ask these questions and that it is normal to have and express such feelings. If necessary, allow the child to express the feeling of rejection, of not being wanted, the feeling of hurt. But also help the child put the matter into perspective by suggesting that it wasn't him/her that was being rejected but the responsibility that the birth mother did not feel ready to accept. It is then, and only then, appropriate for the parent to reassure the child that s/he is loved and wanted by the adoptive parents and is as valued as if born to them. A comment by the mother, such as "I would have been very proud to have had you grow in my body," is appropriate because it is true and because it tends to dilute the child's fantasy of his own undesirability.

Adoptive parents should also recognize, in this connection, that all children, adopted or not, get angry at their parents from time to time and contend with mixed feelings toward them. This has nothing to do with adoption, but, because the parents are in an adoptive situation, they may tend to relate the child's behavior to it. *Adoptive parents need to be aware of the tendency to perceive all their children's experiences through the adoptive lens.* Parents should relate to the feelings the children have without interpreting those feelings as an indictment of them.

Dealing specifically with a child's perceived rejection varies with the individuals involved. Honesty is absolutely essential. Parents should not expect to have a single "right" answer. What is said is less important than the feelings of acceptance behind the words. It is important not to be too critical of the birth mother, as this may invite the child to defend her and hence, to identify too strongly with her. Conversely, it is inadvisable to lavish her with such praise that the child sees her as victimized and distraught over the sacrifice she chose to make.

The middle ground is probably best. The following is an appropriate explanation: "We don't know a great deal about your birth mother, but we do know that she found herself in a difficult position and wanted to make the right decision for you. She wanted you to have a better life than she could provide for you, and she found that, through adoption, you could be given a good home with a mother and father who would love you and care for you as she felt you should be cared for. Having made her decision probably before you were born, she was then in a better position to work out her own situation; she could go back to school, work, or whatever. She made this decision knowing it was final." By emphasizing that the woman probably made her decision prior to the child's birth, the child is less likely to feel that she took a look at her/him and decided s/he was unlovable.

In any explanation, the question of the birth parents' motivation comes up. Some adoptive parents try to reassure the child of his/her loveability by stating that the birth parent made this decision out of love. There is a catch-22 situation here. On the one hand, if the child equates love with the placement decision, s/he may conclude, "You say you love me too—does that mean you'll give me away as well?" On the other hand, if you know the birth parent(s) and are convinced that the love is really there, it would be unfair to avoid saying this. But in either case, the child should know the multiple reasons for placement and should be guaranteed that you will never make the same decision.

The literature on adoption contains many references to the conflicts and identity issues adoptees go through in their developmental years (Triseliotis 1973; Sorosky, Baran, and Pannor 1975). The following describes the situation of a twelve-year-old girl who was particularly troubled by her adoptive status. As the middle child and only adopted child in this family, adoption was used divisively by Donna and other family members. In this interview, Donna expresses the confusion and hurt feelings that many adoptees state has been their experience.

Dr. Smith: I am an adoptive parent—two of my three are adopted. But the two who are adopted outnumber the one who isn't. In your case, it's the other way around. I know your sister, Judy, has said things about your being adopted, but I don't know about your brother, Steve.

Donna: He doesn't say anything.

Dr. Smith: He doesn't say anything, but adoption can be used as a weapon, and like you said, it was sort of like "hitting below the belt" with it—things like, "you know you're not my real sister." If Judy were here, I would say—"Is that the way you feel, that she's not your real sister?" And what do you think she would say?

Donna: I don't think she really means it. I think it's just a way to get back.

Dr. Smith: It comes out when she's angry—is that right?

Donna: Sometimes she says it when she says she's joking around, but she doesn't know how much it really hurts me.

Dr. Smith   Do you tell her it hurts you?

Donna: She would probably say that, well, "why should it hurt you— you're just an adopted kid—why be any different?" I don't know really what she would say, but the way she acts, it's probably what she would say. Or she would say she really didn't care.

Dr. Smith: Does she understand how different it is to be an adopted child?

Donna: I don't really think she does, because I guess, it's just, I guess you have to be an adopted child to understand how it feels. There was this kid in school and everything—everybody was, you know, talking abut me because I was an adopted child. And then one of my friends came over, and said I know how it feels—and I told her she didn't know how it feels because she wasn't an adopted child, she didn't really have the experience or realize the things that happened to me. I can do the same things as any other child, but I kind of feel out of place because I really want to find out what my parents are like. Well, mom found out some things about my parents—my natural parents—though she said I couldn't find out if I had any brothers or sisters at all and she said it was really against the law and all that and I was kind of upset because I really wanted to know if I had any brothers and sisters.

Dr. Smith: I understand what you mean, but if you saw them on the street, what would you really have in common with them? Would you have any feelings for them?

Donna: Probably not as. . . . No, I don't think so.

Dr. Smith: See, love is something that develops over a long period of time, and I guess in a sense it's our hang-up with blood that those relationships were more important. But your mother and father met each other—they probably didn't love each other the first time they saw each other. They may not even have been able to stand each other but the love grew, and I get the feeling that they have a pretty close relationship with each other. I guess you have to decide who are your loved ones. You're smiling.

Donna: Well, I know who my real parents are.

Dr. Smith: Who are your real parents?

Donna: My mom and dad that I live with right now.

Dr. Smith: Do you have feelings about this person who gave you up years ago?

Donna: I would probably, if I really knew her as well as I do my mom and dad, I would probably love her just as much, but I'm kind of wondering why she did give me up and if she really did love me, so I don't know.

Dr. Smith: I don't know if she loved you. I don't know if she didn't. Usually the way these situations go is, it was very difficult. She found herself in a situation she felt she couldn't handle, and she wanted you to have the best kind of family life that anybody could give you, and so she made that decision. But I don't know what her feelings were about that. Do you think your fantasy is that she's hurting over this decision that she made?

Donna: No, I don't really think so.

Dr. Smith: Do you have a fantasy that she is glad about this decision she
              made? What does your fantasy tell you about this woman . . . or
              are you thinking about a woman and a man?

Donna: Well, I'm just wondering what they really look like and what I'm
              really worried about is if they had health problems or anything. . .

Dr. Smith: Health problems?

Donna: Yeah, like I really wanted to know if they had a problem, if they
              ever had a case history of like, some sort of disease and I was
              afraid that they might pass it on to me. Mom and Dad thought that
              I was really trying to get back at them but I wasn't. I just was
              trying to find out if I'd be healthy or if any changes would happen
              to me or if I'd be really tall or I'd be short or something.

Dr. Smith: I think those are very natural questions. Questions about what they
              looked like, how tall they were, what color hair, what color eyes,
              what kind of allergies, what kind of family diseases there were, if
              there was diabetes in the family. Those are all very natural
              questions. Did your parents say they wouldn't be able to get that
              kind of information?

Donna: They didn't say.

Dr. Smith: Well, let me. . . can I talk to them about this. Suppose I tried to get
              some information from the agency, as much as they have and share
              that with you. Would you want me to do that?

Donna: Well, I found some things that my mom brought home.

Dr. Smith: Really?

Donna: Yeah, I found out that my natural mother, not the mother I'm with
              right now, but that she had polio when she was six and mono when
              she was in high school.

Dr. Smith: Mono when she was in high school? Anything else?

Donna: No, I guess not.

Dr. Smith: I think you have a right to this genetic heritage and, you know, to
              the extent that this information is available and if your parents

aren't able to, I can write to the agency, and they can send it to me, and I can share it with you. But, I think what you've got to do is come to terms with the idea that this woman, for whatever reason, made that decision and, I mean, could you live with it? I think it's very unfortunate that adoption can be used as a weapon in a family . . . either by you or by your parents or your brothers or sisters. See, this is not to say that what we do is right, but we have this rule that adoption is not used as a way to get somebody else to do something they don't want to. It's just a standard rule. I mean, two of my kids are adopted. But, so what? That doesn't give them any special privileges, and it doesn't give them any special deficits either. There is no way they can use that to their advantage or disadvantage. We're their parents and they're our children and the way they came to us is almost immaterial. At the same time, it's okay to realize that there's a difference and that's what I want to talk to you about. What are your feelings about being an adopted child? Is it harder, is it more difficult? Do you wish maybe you weren't adopted?

Donna: Well, sometimes when my parents. . . . I guess I just try to get back at them with a little bit of my adoption and I get. . . . I'm sort of happy that they. . . . I think about the reasons like maybe my mother, my natural mother, didn't have too many things like you said, and I'm happy that they did give me somebody who could really care for me better than they could, but sometimes I kind of wonder whether it was really the right choice because I sometimes wonder whether my parents really did love me, and I always say to myself, "Well, I don't know why my natural father and mother had to give me up."

Dr. Smith: It bothers you that the decision was made to give you up?

Donna: Sometimes, some of it.

Dr. Smith: If they hadn't given you up do you have any fantasies of what your life would be like?

Donna: No. I don't know. If . . . I would probably be living. . . . I was born in another city, and I guess I might just live there and might totally live the same way they do . . . and most of the people in my natural family are tall and I don't know. I would probably look more like them, and people wouldn't always be asking why I don't look like my mom and dad and everything.

Dr. Smith: That bugs you when they keep commenting on that, is that right?

Donna: Yeah. I remember one time when this one lady came over to our house. I think she was our piano teacher. I was sitting next to my sister, I mean, next to the piano, listening to her play and then, after the thing the lady came up to me and said, "It's really nice of you to come over and listen to Judy." And then she went over to Judy and said, "You sure have nice friends," and then she said, "She's my sister." And she said, "You don't look a thing like her." That kind of made me upset that I can't look like the rest of my family but I think now I see that nobody really looks exactly like anybody else.

Dr. Smith: I think sometimes people make remarks that do hurt, that are very tactless, that shows their insensitivity. But I don't think they mean to hurt. I think it's what I call our "hang-up with blood." You know, people are always making remarks that "blood is thicker than water," "he's a chip off the old block," "he inherited the personality characteristics of that person." That's only a small part of the story. The fact is, you will turn out to be the kind of person that, within reason, your parents are. Because you are the product of both your heredity and your environment. I guess my question to you is, do you think they love you?

Donna: I really do, but I wonder, I do wonder, I see them, I don't know if it's true but sometimes I see them paying a little more attention to Judy because she's younger and Steve because he's older. I feel kind of like the middle child, like I'm right smack dab in the middle and if I get blamed for anything it's because she's younger and the baby of the family and he's older and he's maturing more, and he's little bit older than I am. I'm right in the middle of those two. And I know they get in trouble as much as I do but I kind of feel that I'm not. . . . I guess it's the same with Judy and Steve. I think Judy feels she's the baby, she doesn't get the same things as I do. I get more. I guess I get more responsibility.

Dr. Smith: Yeah, I agree. In fact, I told your parents this. In some ways you are unique because you are the middle child, okay? And that's rough. It is also rough in that your sister came into the world fourteen months after you did. So you just got used to them and you had to share them. Not that you remember that. But it is also rough being the only adopted child. Now I think it is also important not to use that as some sort of a leverage to either make them prove that they love you as much as they love Judy and Steve. In other words, I think you have got to accept the adoption as a fact of life and ask, "do I really belong to this family?" If you come to that decision, that this is the family you really belong to, then let's forget about adoption. You know, let's go on and live our life and be happy. If communication is a problem between you and your parents, then let's talk about it.

Donna: Well, it's partly my fault because I am usually all by myself. Like on Sunday dinner and we're all together, I usually go off and eat by myself. I'm trying to eat with them but sometimes they bring up subjects or fights and they start fighting right in the middle of it and then I get caught in the fight and everybody gets upset and they bring up things that I don't really want to talk about. They always ask me questions all the time, always suspicious that I'm doing something wrong and I guess . . . I don't know. I guess I'm a loner, I just like being all by myself most of the time. I don't like big groups, being in big groups. When I'm in big groups I don't think I can handle it. I don't like being around a whole lot of people at one time. I know there are only five in my family but I like just sitting by myself and eating. I guess thinking things out by myself or just sitting there by myself for a little while and when I'm talking to my friends I can't have a big crowd around me. I'll talk to one person. Sometimes I just like walking by myself or playing games by myself.

Dr. Smith: I guess what I'm reacting to or what I'm hearing you say is that you do feel by yourself but I also get the flavor of your feeling that you've been abandoned.

Donna: Well, I don't really feel abandoned because it's mostly I go off and do it myself, but . . . .

Dr. Smith: Yeah, but where do you feel you belong? Do you feel like you don't know where you belong?

Donna: It's really like I don't know where I belong. I don't know what. . .

Dr. Smith: And do you think maybe it's because you're struggling with the idea of having been given up?

Donna: I kind of feel like they really didn't want me. It's like, and then I feel like mom and dad felt sorry for seeing a little baby. . . . I don't know. And then I feel kind of privileged because I was among all these other babies, and they picked me out of all of them. That's what everybody says. You know, you're so privileged. It's not really being privileged because you get caught with all the worries and hassles, and they think it's really neat to be adopted because you get the privilege.

Dr. Smith: They don't know that there is a side of being adopted where it hurts, right?

Donna: I guess it's like you have to be there. I mean, it's like you have to have the experience. They think it's so neat and that you're different, you start believing them. And then I guess you start believing yourself you're so different. People think it's so neat to be different so you just try to please them and be different.

Dr. Smith: Do you ever get the message that people say that you should be grateful that they rescued you from a bad situation?

Donna: Yes, because, they say you could have just been left there or something like that or you're lucky.

Dr. Smith: Who says that?

Donna: Well, they ask me like when they found out I was adopted, they said . . . some of my friends said you're very lucky—it's very lucky that you got picked. I mean it's not—they said I was very lucky to be picked by such a nice family. That makes me feel good that they think my family is nice but what makes me so lucky. But is also makes me feel bad, that I had to be saved.

Dr. Smith: Or that you were undesirable? Is that the feeling? Do you ever have the fantasy that your birth mother took one look at you and said, "I don't want this kid?"

Donna: That's what I thought at first.

Dr. Smith: At first?

Donna: But, I guess it's been with me ever since I was a child. I guess I've had that feeling.

Dr. Smith: What if I told you that in all probability, and I think this is the case, in all probability she made her decision before you were even born. In other words, she could not have seen you, but that it was the situation she found herself in that she felt she wanted to make a decision that was going to be helpful to you.

Donna: I remember thinking to myself and I said maybe she—I asked my mom and dad if they had become like, like she was going to give me up in the first place like when she was during her pregnancy and mom and dad just got me back, like before. But then I realized that I wasn't. . . . they hadn't really talked to the mother or anything or talked to anybody and they told me they didn't, they got me just out of seeing and, so, I thought maybe she just wanted to give me up because . . . I really can't explain it but like . . . just like you said, like she took one look at me. . . .

Dr. Smith: That's your fantasy; she took one look at you?

Donna: I don't know if it's a fantasy. Some of the time I wish that, it's true, I have to be honest with you, sometimes I do wish she hadn't really given me up. I wish she had really taken me. Sometimes I really wish that for a small while I could spend a little time with her. If I did that, I know I'd be hurting my mom and dad, and I really don't want to do that, I really don't. I really think they love me too much.

Dr. Smith: And at the same time, it hurts you that she gave you up. . . .

Donna: I probably will never see her.

Dr. Smith: In other words, that you are really experiencing a rather severe loss. You feel you lost something.

Donna: Yes, I remember one time I was talking to my friend, and I told her I had two sets of parents . . . that it was really neat that I could go see sometime I could go see my other parents and spend time with them, but then I knew it wasn't true. I knew I could never see them.

Dr. Smith: I think you should know that all adopted children wonder what these people are like, what they look like, what they are as people; because part of what you are is tied up with them. Now, I think that at some point in your life you will be able to decide, you know, if you actually want to look them up. What I advise people to do, and I tell my own kids this, too, you know, that's an important decision that only you can make when the time comes. But, you know, it's one thing to be so curious and having that need that's so great that if you go to look them up, are you willing to face the consequences, whatever that is. In other words, this mother may not want to see you and may be upset with that visit. She may say, "Well, I don't know who you are," she may deny the whole thing, or she may say, "Well, I did have a child but the child has her own home, her own family, and I look at you as a total stranger." You know, that's why I think a lot of adoptees feel that, look, a decision has been made which supposedly was in my best interest. Why upset the decision that she made, you know, twenty years ago? I am not trying to talk you into it or out of it, Donna, I think that there are things to be said on both sides. And I am also saying that I can see where that part of the experience hurt. And I think growing up is hard regardless of whether you're adopted or not.

Donna: I guess it would really be up to her because I guess it was her decision in what she decided. I guess I'd have to live with that. Since I have to live with that, I guess I'll have to cope with it and I'll have to work it out and I guess with the help of my family I really can work it out and I won't use it as a weapon against my family as an excuse. But it's just like trying to quit smoking . . . it takes time.

Dr. Smith: You know what I also see in your eyes? I see a lot of hurt that the decision was made. I think that kind of hurt is natural. I am sorry you hurt, Donna. And, I'm sorry people have used adoption as a weapon against you, and I am sorry you had to feel that you had to use it to throw a dig at your parents. But nobody can say that you have to belong to this family. I think that's a decision you have to make. "Who are my real parents? Are my real parents the ones who brought me into the world or are my real parents the ones who cared for me, nurtured me, cried over me when I was sick . . . who are my real parents?" And, that's a decision you will have to make.

Donna: I guess the definition of parents is what you said, really taking care
           of me. That makes me feel good.

This case illustrates the mixture of feelings that many adoptees verbalize. The first thing it highlights is the tremendous variation in responses and reactions adoptees experience, and there is no body of knowledge that presupposes a universality of response. Secondly, even though this family was somewhat typical of other adoptive families, it was unfortunate that adoption was allowed to be used as a weapon, both by family members and by Donna herself. The reader may be interested in knowing that Donna has now accepted her place in her "new" family but that before she was able to do so, she had to (belatedly) work through the angry and struggling feelings with which she was contending. Also, the rules for allowing her to isolate herself from her family have been altered so that this behavior is no longer allowed. In essence, both she and other family members have truly accepted Donna's real place in the family.

In some cases, the problems of youngsters require more than educationally focused reading or lecturing material. What you have just read was an actual case involving a moderately disturbed young lady. The psychologist who tested her had this to say:

In her responses on the Thematic Appreception Test, she pictures her main characters as impulsive and directly aggressive. There are a number of themes of violence in her fantasy and indications that she may be a repressor of hostility. She offers a fairly negative view of male/female relationships and pictures families as distant and uncaring. There are indications that Donna is indeed concerned about self-identity, including one very interesting tale of a "transplant" of organs from one person to another. There also appear to be indicators of concern about herself as a baby and what happened to her then. This may well be related to a lack of resolution of the adoption issue. There are themes of a wish for reconciliation but it is unclear whether this would be with her biological family or more in reference to the perceived problem in Donna's present circumstance.

In another situation, nine-year-old Teri was tested by the psychologist, and her responses suggested a perception of the world as a confused and ungiving place. They further indicated little hope for good in the future. She docs not anticipate positive interactions with others and presents herself in an emotionally guarded and distant fashion. With low self-esteem, she regards herself unfavorably as compared to her peers.

This child was admitted to a treatment program designed to work through her feelings of maternal abandonment. (Indeed, she was not placed into her pre-adoptive home until she was seven years old.) Letting go of her biological mother, emotionally, and replacing her with her new mother represented a major therapeutic task. In therapy, it was nearly impossible to get her in touch with feelings about her birth mother's rejection, stating only, "I feel she did the best she was able to do." She never was able to see the connection between her denial of feelings and her rejection of the preadoptive mother.

Often the line between "normal" problem behaviors and the need for "therapy" is imperceptible. The following case illustrates a sequence of events that provides new light when seen through the adoptive lens. They are issues related to (perceived) abandonment, rejection, and anger.

Jim and Sue Lockport leased a horse for their fourteen-year-old (adopted) daughter, Megan. At first, Megan was wary of the horse, keeping herself at a distance, petting the horse, but only when invited to do so. Gradually, she became closer and closer to the horse, looking forward to riding it, and before too long, began to refer to it as "my horse."

One evening she overheard a conversation between her parents, the essence of which was a plan not to follow through on purchasing the horse as the father felt it was a bit too spirited for the family taste. Instead, they would let the lease run out and look for another horse for Megan. At that moment, the girl rushed into the bedroom, flew into a rage and, with tears rolling down her cheeks, demanded to know how he could do such a thing as to give her horse away, as she put it. The parents tried to explain the basis of their thinking but remained steadfast in their plan. Megan cried herself to sleep that evening.

The following week, when the family was visiting Megan's horse, the father noticed how uninvolved Megan was with the horse. In contrast with the previous week, when she was hugging and kissing the horse, Megan barely made contact, petting her only occasionally. It was obvious to all that Megan was protecting herself by this distancing maneuver.

Of course, one could argue that this incident was not adoption-related, but the sheer overreaction on Megan's part lends credence to the conclusion that her sensitivity to the "giving away" process was a bit overdone and had some real personal meaning to her.

In summary, the adopted child in latency has already introduced his/her parents to some of the conflicts to be faced during adolescence. This is a time to forge ahead with a new and renegotiated relationship that can have lasting repercussions and significance.

Chapter 9

The Adopted Adolescent

Scanning the literature on the issues inherent in adolescence for adoptees can prove a Herculean task. Even without adoption, because of the massive hormonal surges of that age, adolescence is a troublesome time of life when self-doubts and searching questions are the rule. For the adopted teen, the problems of searching for one's identity are exacerbated in situations where his/her relationship with the parents is strained and/or his/her identification with them is tentative or incomplete.

In introducing the subject of adolescence in my human development course, I usually confide to my students that I cannot discuss the subject without breaking into a cold sweat. Conventional wisdom maintains that mood swings and temper outbursts are fairly typical in contemporary family life. But in the human-service community, which includes psychiatrists, psychologists, and social workers, the view prevails that such symptomatology is usually a manifestation of preexisting family related problems heightened and intensified in adolescence. One of my mentors in my doctoral program at the University of Chicago (Daniel Offer, MD) carried out a research study of "normal" adolescents and found that the turbulence attributed to this phase to be highly exaggerated (1969).

That period of life we refer to as adolescence is fraught with mixed feelings for both the adolescent as well as his/her parents. To the adolescent it represents, on the one hand, an end of parental domination or at least a

The writer is indebted to his daughter, Sandra L. Applebaum, MD, for her assistance in writing this chapter.

diminution of parental control, but conversely it calls for increased responsibility and decision-making regarding future roles and goals (which in and of itself produces considerable anxiety). At the same time, s/he views this period of life with a certain mystique and intrigue regarding his/her own future romantic life and experiences. This, too, arouses both pleasure and apprehension. Parents whose children have reached the adolescent years wonder how stormy the familial environment will become and muse over the implications that a son or daughter is now a "man" or "woman." As James Anthony accurately pointed out, if the adult remembers how much of her/himself went into the making of an adolescent, s/he would be better able to understand the complexities of the changed relationship between parent and adolescent (1969). The matter was well summarized by a Hebrew sage in 1230: "Your son at five is your master, at ten your slave, at fifteen your double, and after that, your friend or foe, depending on how you brought him up." In short, the period we refer to as adolescence that symbolically represents a rite of passage from childhood, is viewed by all ages with both positive and negative feelings. Certainly in the light of our "sexual revolution," there are grounds for concerns about adolescent renunciation of traditional personal and family sexual values and standards.

Many adolescents turn to literature as a way of expressing and reflecting their confused and, at times, tormented state of existence. But not all adolescents experience the sense of turbulence that the literature would have us believe is universal. Many view this time with a mixture of sorrow and joy, anxieties and expectations. One young man, in thinking about these transitory years, stated:

> Before me stood the massive, three-story building complex with its maze of unexplored halls, its musty-smelling shops, its gym, its band rooms, and huge auditorium. And here I stood ten years ago, one lonely, insecure, terrified twelve-year-old boy facing his first day at junior-high school. My former warm, secure, sheltered, and protected social matrix which revolved around home, school, neighborhood, and church would, in the near future, be rapidly replaced by an impersonal, demanding, competitive, and often lonely matrix where only the strongest survive and where I would be forced to cope with and adjust to pressures and expectations in order to avoid being bypassed by the system. This one day in my life—my first day as a junior high school student—stands out in my mind as a signpost symbolizing the rites of passage from childhood to adolescence and marked the first step in the gradual maturational process which eventually leads to adulthood. (Author unknown)

This is a time of life that should be viewed as transitional rather than one characterized by behavior that remains fixed. Adolescence is essentially an in-between stage, with no special rights and privileges of its own, and is characterized by the need to examine and re-examine what adolescent's purpose and destiny in life is meant to be.

Parents should realize that the adolescent is primarily a child, not an adult, except in a biological sense. Emotionally s/he is still as dependent on his/her parents as always. However, hormonal changes and societal demands propel him/her to claim her/his independence and to make assertions that probably can never be met. The wise parent would do well not to force the youngster to carry out his/her claims. The parent should always allow the young person to retreat and save face, recognizing that we have all spoken foolishly and irresponsibly from time to time.

Another characteristic of the adolescence phenomena is extreme idealism. The adolescent finds the adult world full of contradictions. For those adolescents who have observed inconsistencies in behaviors of parents or adults which do not jibe with their avowed stances, his/her own value framework may be undergoing change and heightened anxiety. The way s/he may deal with such conflicts is to identify even more with a group of peers who, s/he perceives, are experiencing similar phenomena with their own parents.

The transition from childhood to adulthood may be a rather sudden shift, or it may occur gradually in a setting where children and adults are not sharply separated groups. In situations or societies in which children and adults constitute clearly defined groups, the adolescent does not wish to belong any longer to the children's group and at the same time s/he knows that s/he is not really accepted in the adult group. In this case s/he has a position similar to what is called in sociology the "marginal man."

To discuss adolescence in its widest ramifications, that is, physiologically, metabolically, psychologically, anthropologically, developmentally, etc., is beyond the scope of this book. However, one writer has added such insights into our understanding, particularly relevant to the adoptive situation, that his genius cannot be ignored. One of the most prolific writers of our day, Erik Erikson has illuminated our understanding of the adolescent (as well as other phases of development). Erikson added the dimension of cultural influences on personality within an already existing sophisticated psychoanalytic perspective. His contributions, it seems, complement rather than supplant psychoanalytic theory, which further speaks to his genius.

According to Erikson, the central problem of the adolescent is the establishment of a sense of identity. The identity the adolescent seeks to clarify is his own: who is he and what is his role in society to be? Is he a child or an adult? Does he have the wherewithal to be a good husband and father some day? Will his race or religion prevent him from reaching his tentative goals? Overall, will he be a success or failure? Because of the questions he poses to himself, the adolescent is sometimes morbidly preoccupied with how he appears in the eyes of others and how he can make the roles and skills he has learned earlier conform with current styles.

Perhaps because of our success-oriented culture, Erikson states, it is the inability to select an appropriate occupational identity that most disturbs young people:

> To keep themselves together they temporarily over-identify, to the point of apparent complete loss of identity, with the heroes of cliques and crowds. On the other hand, they become remarkably clannish, intolerant and cruel in their exclusion of others who are "different," in skin color or cultural background . . . arbitrarily as *the* signs of an in-grouper or out-grouper. It is important to understand such intolerance as the necessary defense against a sense of identity diffusion, which is unavoidable at a time of life when the body changes its proportions radically . . . when intimacy with the other sex approaches and is, on occasion, forced on the youngster, and when life lies before one with a variety of conflicting possibilities and choices. Adolescents help one another temporarily through such discomfort by forming cliques and by stereotyping themselves, their ideals, and their enemies. (Erikson 1963, 218-219).

Viewed from this perspective in a culture that extols, above all other considerations, "success," the compensatory drives of adolescence can readily be understood. To the adolescent, what represents strength takes precedence over what is evidence of true or mature strength. The adolescent needs to feel powerful, to obliterate all possible rivals, and to rely for such purposes on fantasies of omnipotence.

Summarizing the phenomenon of adolescence is a monumental task, but I best like the statement of Anna Freud. She stated:

> I take it that it is normal for an adolescent to behave for a considerable length of time in an inconsistent and unpredictable manner; to fight his impulses and to accept them; to ward them off successfully and to be overrun by them; to love his parents and to hate them; to revolt against them and to be dependent on them; to be deeply ashamed to acknowledge his mother before others and, unexpectedly, to desire heart to heart talks with her; to thrive on imitation of and identification with others while searching unceasingly for his own identity; to be more idealistic, artistic, generous, and unselfish than he will ever be again, but also the opposite: self-centered, egotistic, calculating. Such fluctuations between extreme opposites would be deemed highly abnormal at any other time of life. At this time they may signify no more than that an adult structure of personality takes a long time to emerge, that the ego of the individual in question does not cease to experiment and is in no hurry to close down on possibilities. If the temporary solutions seem abnormal to the onlooker, they are less so, nevertheless, than the hasty decisions made in other cases for one-sided suppression, or revolt, or flight, or withdrawal, or regression, or asceticism, which are responsible for the truly pathological development described above. (1958, 275-276).

If adolescents living with their biological parents suffer from a crisis of identity, the confusion faced by the adopted child is compounded because he now knows he has birth parents. The genealogical questions become paramount as he learns about reproduction and childbearing, particularly at a time in our history when we understand better the genetic aspects of functioning, as, for example, a propensity for depression. Reactions to adolescence may vary with adoptees, as with all adolescents. He may deny the existence of some traits he believes are inherited. The degree to which he works out such conflicts is directly related to the success the adoptive parents have had in conveying the message that he is one of them in every sense of the word; that is, the entitlement issue has been adequately resolved.

The adolescent adoptee has a legitimate right to question her/his ancestral roots. Such questioning does not imply that the parents have somehow failed the child. It is characteristic of all adolescents, adopted *and* biological, to question and even reject parental standards in preference to peer standards. Parents should face this behavior with a calm willingness to discuss anything of concern to the adolescent. Keeping the lines of communication open is vital to the healthy resolution of some of the universal interpersonal tensions characteristic of the adolescent years.

If the adolescent has questions about genetic or hereditary characteristics, and if the adoptive parents have access to such knowledge, they should make the information available to him/her without hesitation or trepidation. If information is not available, great efforts should be made to find some. Generally, the adolescent is curious about what his/her birth parents looked like and what kind of lifestyles they led, rather than names, place, and date of birth, etc.

Ultimately, conflicts do arise, and tension is inevitable. Arguments over whether the adoptive or birth parents are the "real" parents can be used as a weapon by either the adolescent or the parent. Children may use any weapons available to them in battles with their parents. The adopted child simply has one more in his arsenal. When the adolescent strikes out angrily, saying, "I don't have to listen to you, you aren't my real parents anyway," the most appropriate response may be to let the matter drop without further comment (but not give in). Then, when cooler heads prevail, comment on the use made by your adolescent of the fact of adoption. This form of metacommunication, that is, an analysis of the nature of communication between two people, can be quite valuable in averting future nonproductive encounters. You might say, "We have cared for you as if you were our birth child, and our feelings for you are the same as if you had been born to us. We will not let you use the adoption as a way to control us. We don't use it, and we don't feel it is fair for you to use it." Such communication lets the adolescent know that his/her feelings are understandable and that his relationship with his/her parents is a special one. The message reaffirms that s/he is, indeed, the adopted parents' child.

The handling of such volatile situations is extremely important. Resolution of such issues, in my point of view, depends upon the preexisting relationship between adoptive parents and their children. It is crucial that such a potentially explosive situation be handled with honesty and sincerity. By adolescence, the child's power of perception is acute. Because adolescents are sensitive to mixed messages, insincerity, and hypocrisy, it is vital that the adoptive parent recognize his/her own feelings before attempting to reassure the child about his/her origins. For example, any feelings of competitiveness and/or anger (even envy) should be acknowledged to oneself. If not acknowledged, these feelings will emerge in your communication with the adolescent: there is no way to disguise it.

Adopters invariably ask the child-care experts about adoptees' searches for their birth parents. Parents should realize that interest on the part of their children to find out more about their heritage may be a function of mixed and often multiple motivations. Some are curious only about looks and physical characteristics of birth parents, as well as disease proneness. Others are obsessed with the notion of their genetic forebears, and their interest is tied to a need to determine one's psychological identity. Parents should recognize that it is only natural for adolescents to wonder who they look like and, having missed out on this opportunity, to once again ask the question, "Why?"

For years, the field was immersed in a controversy about searches. The public perception is that all adopted people search. Brodzinsky supported this perception when he stated that 100 percent of adoptees search (1992). He then went on to explain that his definition of "search" included any sort of questioning the adoptee asks about his/her origins. The fact is that only a handful (judging from inquiries from states where this is an allowed practice) actually do.

There is no doubt that there has been movement in this area. One compromise between pressures to know and the need for privacy has been the establishment of mutual consent registries. Twenty-four states have established such registries (Pierce and Adamec 1991).

Adoptees' Handling of Feelings

Earlier in this book, I made reference to adoptive parents' use of denial, more or less along the lines of Kirk's denial of difference concept. But adults are not the only ones who use this primitive defense (which actually protects us from dealing with the impact of strong feelings).

Recently, a colleague and I conducted a workshop called "Coping and Living with Adoption," and we invited a panel of adopted adolescents to address the group on the subject of what the adoption experience meant to them, personally and subjectively. One was a fifteen-year-old, a bright, achieving, determined youngster, who manifested this same trait of splitting off her feelings from her thinking.

> "I've grown up all my life knowing I'm adopted, so I have no problems with it. Kids sometimes ask about my being adopted and I tell them, 'Yes, it's okay to be adopted, and that is something that makes me feel special.'" (As this young lady was talking about her adoptive status, it became clear to the audience that she was having a hard time remaining cool, objective, and unemotional. To the audience, it became clear that other emotions were bubbling to the surface, as her voice began to quiver, words were hard to articulate, and tears were streaming down her cheeks.)

Recognizing this discrepancy between the spoken word and the emotional expression, I asked, "But how hard is it to be adopted?" She regained a little of her composure, reiterated her basic stance that it wasn't hard; she knows she is loved by her family and that it is all right to talk about the transition from birth to adoptive family. Now the tears really began to flow, and the audience was in tune to the pain she was feeling *about being given up.* This experience helped her to tie together the intellectual reaction of being wanted and loved (by her adoptive family) and being given up (by her birth family).

Another adoptee, now in her twenties, related her experience in another way:

Amy: I've always had this sense that I'm not quite the person that my (adoptive) mother wants me to be.

Dr. Smith: Would she say that there was a disappointment that you didn't turn out quite right?

Amy: I doubt it.

Dr. Smith: In fact, she would say she is quite proud of how you turned out.

Amy: True.

Dr. Smith: When you were dating, did you tell dates that you were adopted?

Amy: Yes, when it came up, but I never made a special point to tell my dates.

Dr. Smith: How about your husband? At what point in your courtship did you reveal this to him?

Amy: Probably early in the relationship, but I don't remember exactly.
              We started dating about seven months after my father died, and I
              remember we had some serious discussions about personal things,
              so it may have come up at that point.

Dr. Smith: How hard is loss for you?

Amy: Hard. It's always been hard.

Dr. Smith: Are there things about your birth family you don't know but would
              like to know?

Amy: I'm going through a struggle right now, because I want to connect
              up with my birth mother, but I'm told by my intermediary that she
              is not interested in meeting with me.

Dr. Smith: How is her reaction for you?

Amy: Hard. Real hard. Because I know she has a family, is now married,
              and has four other children. Now those are my siblings, or at least
              half-siblings, and I do feel cheated. I'm hurt, and I do feel angry
              about that.

In another case situation, fourteen-year-old Denise found herself as the
only adopted child in her family (three older biological children in this family).
Her projective drawings suggested a strong need to present a happy contented
portrayal of her family and her life. However, Denise seems to struggle with
feelings of insecurity and has a tendency toward guardedness and evasiveness.
She is likely to act out with impulsive aggressiveness when things do not go her
way and may display inadequate control of her emotions. She seems to feel that
her environment imposes unnecessary limitations on her life, as in her house
drawing, which shows her living in her own "little house" connected to her
parents' home. Thus, while she appears to be struggling with desires for
independence and autonomy, she continues to feel dependent upon her parents
at the same time, in this typical adolescent struggle. Denise appears to be
strongly concerned with outward appearances, focusing on brand labels people
are wearing on their clothing. This seems to be a typical adolescent response
that may relate to her sense of identity, feeling of belonging within her peer
group, and her sense of self-esteem. Feelings of sadness, trauma, and
hopelessness are suggested in these drawings also and may relate to unresolved
feelings concerning her adoption.

During the family therapy session, Denise felt powerless in the face of her parents and her therapist. She shut down at a point when she felt all the adults in the room were against her. She now claims that she needs to do this in order to gain some semblance of control over mounting anger. She also admitted that "it's no fun being in the hot seat," that it leaves her feeling exposed and vulnerable. She also verbalized that she does not think her parents understand her feelings despite their well-meaning intentions.

The individual session went something like the following:

Dr. Smith: Denise, do I understand you?

Denise: In some ways I think you do, but in some ways, you don't, but I have to say that I don't understand myself, so it's a mixed bag.

Dr. Smith: To what extent do you want me to understand you?

Denise: Not totally—because I'm afraid that I will lose control, and I am afraid that I'll get too violent. I have a violent nature, and that scares me, so I'd kind of like to keep a lid on things, fearing things that are way down there that I don't want to come up.

Dr. Smith: I'm not going to go excavating for those deep hidden layers. But tell me this. There are really two of you. One is this fun-loving person, the outgoing, gregarious, life of the party that everyone wants to be near, but when this presentation doesn't work, you feel lonely, abandoned, and ultimately engage in self-destructive behaviors. So my question is this. Are there some feelings of guilt about the fact that this lady, out of her pain over not being able to care for you, made this ultimate sacrifice in giving you up, so you could have all the things she wasn't able to give you?

Denise: (A pause.) I never thought about it that way before, but you might have something there, because I always wind up feeling guilty whether it's something I do or don't do.

Dr. Smith: Then you'll have to ask yourself how reasonable these feelings are and really struggle with them.

What is revealed by this young person can be universalized to the adoptive experience, and is heightened and manifested during the tumultuous adolescent years. The feelings involve loss, rejection, acceptability, guilt, control, and identity.

Adolescence and Open Adoption

Lois Melina and Sharon Kaplan (1993) have provided the field with a number of scenarios about how the openness concept can affect members of the triad. For some adopted adolescents, the openness may bring some peace of mind and resolution. For others, it may prolong the conflict and be an invitation to add another dimension to an existing problematic relationship between the adoptee and his/her parents. These authors do an excellent job in highlighting problems related to insecurity, family identification, ambivalent loyalties, identity, and surges for independence. While I do not have the experience to offer specific guidelines in such cases, it seems to me that a professional person connected to an agency plays a potentially greater role in offering services related to mediation, support, and clarification. And here I must underscore what has been stated repeatedly throughout this book. We do not know how the arrangements will work out. As the research continues, answers will be forthcoming to determine what situations are best suited for openness, semiopenness, and confidentiality, what personality ingredients in adoptive parents and birth parents, that is, the mix in these two families as they interplay in helping the adoptee fashion an identity that will help him/her crystallize an identity that will lead to personal fulfillment in life.

On the issue of co-parenting in a fully disclosed adoption with continued visitation and involvement, while the literature maintains that the adoptive parents are the psychological parents, and the birth parents are viewed as extended family or special friends, this may be no more than hair-splitting. It all depends on the child and his/her phenomenological framework. The familial identification may be with either family or a mixture of both. If with the birth family, are there guilt feelings for not showing a greater appreciation to the adoptive family? If with the adoptive family, are there special feelings, guilt or otherwise, that results in an internalized conflict? These are but some of the questions that must be answered in the future.

Summary

The thing to remember about adolescence is that it is a difficult time of life. Having made the transition, which is often imperceptible, from latency to adolescence, the adoptee carries with him the continuation of the questions posed at that time. Questions such as: who am I and how did I get here; to whom do I belong and/or owe my allegiance; who looks like me, and do I have siblings out there somewhere; and most importantly, will I be able to make it on my own?

Finally, one should remember that studies thus far reveal that adopted adolescents placed during infancy and who have perceived themselves to have been loved do quite well compared with their nonadopted counterparts. For those adolescents who manifest problems in behavior, it is usually not due to the fact of adoption, but to confounding clinical circumstances, such as family breakdown and dysfunctionality.

Chapter 10

Transracial Adoption: Success or Failure?

Transracial adoption—almost exclusively the adoption of nonwhite children with Caucasian families—is a hotly contested child welfare issue.

The modern practice of adoption developed on the principle that every child needs and deserves a family. Child placing agencies used the matching principle that adoption should imitate nature as a way to ensure a successful placement. This meant that black children were placed in black homes, and white children were placed in white homes. That a time should ever come to cross this racial barrier was considered anathema to the best interests of the child, another shibboleth of sound child welfare practice.

For the most part, white adoptive families were able to keep pace with the need for placeable, healthy children, but with the end of World War II and the beginning of the civil rights movement, attention was focused on minority group children for whom adoptive families were not always available. Spurred in part by adoptive parent groups, agencies were forced to focus attention on adoptive resources for these children, one resource being white homes for black children.

During the early and middle 1960s the number of transracial adoptions was small and was virtually unnoticed. However, the end of the decade brought a rapid increase, and the number of transracial adoptions tripled between 1968 and 1971. By 1971, 35 percent of all agency placements of black children were with white families (Ladner 1977).

Recognizing the inequity of needy black children and the scarcity of black families with whom to place them, and encouraged by the changing societal attitude toward civil rights, these placements represented a view that love and affection within a family would transcend racial boundaries. The Child Welfare League of America (CWLA) is a national, voluntary, standard-setting organization in the child welfare field that reflects the field's views on agency and professional practice. In the past twenty-five years, it has changed its position on this practice. In the 1968 edition of *Standards for Adoption Service,* the position of the agency was that "racial background should not determine the selection of the home for a child . . . not be assumed that difficulties will naturally arise if adoptive parents and children are of different racial origin."

In 1972, the standard was revised to recommend making in-racial placement a priority. In 1978, the tone was the same but added the consideration of transracial placement as a means of finding a permanent home for an awaiting child. In 1988, the standard stated:

> Children in need of adoption have a right to be placed into a family that reflects their ethnicity or race. Children should not have their adoption denied or significantly delayed, however, when adoptive parents of other ethnic or racial groups are available (34).

The early 1970s brought all kinds of changes (revolutions would be a better word) in the adoption field. It was at this time that the famous (or infamous, depending on your point of view) *Stanley vs. Illinois* case was decided by the U.S. Supreme Court, enunciating the rights of birth fathers. In 1973 the U.S. Supreme Court legalized abortions, and 1972 brought a screeching halt to transracial adoptions. In a strong denunciation of transracial adoptions, the National Association of Black Social Workers (NABSW) went on record to state the following:

> The NABSW has taken a vehement stand against the placement of Black children in white homes for any reason. We affirm the inviolable position of Black children in Black families where they belong physically, psychologically, and culturally in order that they receive the total sense of themselves and develop a sound projection of their future. Black children in white homes are cut off from the healthy development as Black people, which development is the normal expectation and only true humanistic goal.

Numerous reasons are cited for such opposition. It is believed that transracial adoptions threaten the development of ethnic pride and self-identification so necessary for normal development. Speaking with strong emotion, Edmund Jones stated:

> Black families build in mechanisms to handle living in a racist society. White families could not provide these for a black child. . . . I question the ability of white parents—no matter how deeply imbued with good will—to grasp the

totality of the problem of being black in our society—I question their ability to create what I believe is crucial for these youngsters—a black identity. (Jones 1972, 157)

Questions have also been raised about the motives of white families. Some accusations are along the lines of white paternalism or as a payment of guilt for the racist attitudes in a society of which we are all a part. Some have argued that transracial adoptions are simply a way for white agencies to continue their adoption business as usual—avoiding the black community. Agencies, it is claimed, perpetuate the myth that blacks don't adopt—an argument that is not supported by the research when one controls for economic status. By perpetuating this myth, agencies can continue their practice of ignoring the black community, a charge that agencies refute, by and large.

Many agencies charge that the position of NABSW is highly emotional and not based on actual findings. While the rhetoric may have been toned down over the years, the strong opposition has not abated one iota. The issue, state many agencies, is not whether a child is better off in a black or white home. Nobody argues that black homes are preferable to white homes for a black child. The issue is whether a child is better off in a white home or in a foster care home or institutional setting in which no family identity, black, white, or otherwise, can realistically emerge. Joyce Ladner, a black sociologist, discussed the NABSW position in an article that appeared in *Ebony*:

> They're (NABSW) still unalterably opposed to transracial adoption. . . . But I don't think you'll find anyone who will agree it's better for a black child to remain in an institution rather than in a white home. . . . I just can't believe that (an institution) is better than a white home.

The NABSW, in response to the charges that they would rather see a child go to no home versus a white home, denied advocating such a position, but added that there is not only evidence, but overwhelming evidence that special projects undertaken by agencies to recruit and locate black families can be successful.

The controversy over transracial placements has led to a number of research efforts. Grow and Shapiro carried out a descriptive study of 125 children in transracial placements. A wide range of topics was covered: the general family situation, the neighborhood, the parents' social and racial attitudes, their contacts with blacks and black culture, and the degree of parental satisfaction with the adoption. A major focus was the child's behavior and adjustment with attention to his or her racial awareness and identity.

Identity is an elusive construct, not easily lending itself to an operational definition. One researcher who has come closest to a working definition is Joan Shireman, a professor at Portland State College. She states that identity includes the sense of who I am. It includes the ideas of (1) seeing oneself as a separate person, seeing oneself in relation to others, (2) having one's own unique set of values and ethics on which life and actions are based, and (3) self-esteem. (Shireman 1988, 7)

Of the children in the Grow and Shapiro study, 77 percent were rated successful—a rate comparable to conventional in-racial adoption outcome studies. Children in the largest family units and children that perceived their adoptive parents as obviously black were more likely to have high success scores. The variable "acknowledgment of differences" was a critical factor. The researchers noted that parents who acknowledged their child's racial difference appeared to have had greater ego strength than parents who tended to deny such differences (Grow and Shapiro 1977).

Simon and Altstein interviewed some 200 transracial families. Their purpose was to learn more about the racial attitudes of the children as well as their siblings. Unlike the Grow and Shapiro study, they interviewed the children as well as the parents. They concluded that adopted black children perceived themselves to be black as accurately as white children perceived themselves to be white. They cautioned, however, that since the children were relatively young (in the three-to-eight-year age group), it was too early to tell the strength of their racial identity into adolescence (Simon and Altstein 1977).

A follow-up study some seven years later (with 70 percent of the original sample located), using data collected only from the parents, revealed a high level of satisfaction with the adopted children. However, nearly one-fourth of the parents indicated the presence of problems greater than they had anticipated (Simon and Altstein 1981).

In yet another follow-up, the researchers identified a good deal of continuity from previous findings relative to parent-child relationships and accuracy of racial identities. By now the children were adolescents (Simon and Altstein 1987).

Similar findings are reported by McRoy and Zurcher (1983), who compared the experiences of thirty black teens placed in black homes and thirty in white homes. Both groups reported typical adolescent relationships with parents, siblings, teachers, and peers, and positive feelings of self-regard. The most significant conclusion was that the quality of the parent-child relationship was the key, regardless of the inracial/transracial nature of the placement.

A study conducted by Silverman and Feigelman (1983) revealed similar findings on adjustment outcome. But in comparing those youngsters who were doing well with those who were not, the most critical variable was age at placement. As expected, those who were older at placement were found to be at greatest risk for behavioral problems.

Shireman, in 1988, reported the outcomes of over 100 children of Afro-American descent placed in adoptive homes by two Chicago agencies. The children were under two years of age when placed and followed up periodically over a period of thirteen years, examining indices of intelligence, identity, and school adjustment. She found the same percentage of difficulties in family relationships between inracial and transracial placements (11 percent). A somewhat higher proportion of the transracially adopted children (one-third) were having academic difficulties than the in-racial group (one-fifth), which she attributed to medical difficulties or to negative labeling in the predominantly white schools the children attended. For all the groups, the percentage of problem-free behaviors was 70 percent.

In summary, we find that transracial adoption is a very controversial practice; emotions run high, but it is necessary to separate the objective findings from the emotionality. Basically, the practice boils down to two points of view: (1) the practice should be outlawed because white adoptive parents cannot equip a black youngster with the psychosocial survival mechanisms for living in a racist society, and (2) love is color blind, and children need love, affection, and a feeling of family identity to succeed in life.

Being the cautious, conservative person that I am, I see an element, or several elements, missing from the research. I think we should heed the caveats enunciated by black professionals about potential dangers that lurk down the developmental road. The subjects in these various studies are young teenagers, at best, and they are typically not into later adolescence when dating relationships become more common. For those youngsters who are biracial, there may be an even greater problem of determining, both in their hearts and in their minds, the precise nature of their racial identity (to the extent that this is possible). For example, I have witnessed talk shows featuring two sisters, both biracial, having the same father and mother, where one defines her racial identity as black and dates blacks exclusively, and the other defines her racial identity as white chooses to date both white and black.

The problem in developing a policy that would address the needs of the population one is seeking to serve is that there are many individual cases where a practice may or may not work. As a child advocate, I believe that the practice of transracial adoption should be considered as an option *as long as* the research continues to show that children of transracial families seem to be thriving in them. Even the most diehard opponent of transracial adoption would agree that a home, even a white home, is better than no home. At the same time, agencies should continue their efforts to reach out to recruit black families and to get the word out that bureaucratic policies have been considerably relaxed. For those agencies who continue the practice of transracial adoption, special efforts should be made to educate families about maintaining the black child's ties with other black families through community contacts, such as school and church. We must, as a society, do all we can to relieve the glut of thousands of children languishing in foster homes and institutions. To do anything less than this is professional irresponsibility at its finest.

Chapter 11

The Birth Parents

The key to any adoption is the agreement of the birth parents to relinquish their rights to the child they brought into the world. The field has never truly acknowledged the emotional price to be exacted, short-term and long-term, for having made that decision.

Years ago, when an unmarried pregnant woman came to an agency for help in dealing with her situation, placement of the baby became the obvious choice. Those were the days when out-of-wedlock pregnancy was a stigma-laden experience, the days of maternity homes, when birth fathers' rights were nonexistent. Counseling under these circumstances consisted of taking down information about heights, weights, educational levels in the family, as well as diseases known to exist in the family. It was assumed that the baby would be given up for adoption, and that the birth mother could put this event behind her. The entire field was wearing blinders, seemingly blind to the long-term consequences.

Traditionally, agencies turned to a psychological perspective in understanding some of the reasons and forces underlying a pregnancy outside of marriage. Although it obviously represented a breakdown in the moral code, social workers nevertheless tended to look at the girl/young woman in these circumstances as "sick" rather than "bad." This is hardly surprising; since the 1920s, the field tended to look to the behavioral sciences as ways to understand rather than judge human behavior. The social workers identified her own mother and the strained relationship she experienced with her as the sole causal factor. Typical is the statement of a prominent psychiatrist:

> We feel that the unmarried mother becomes so in an attempt to maintain an
> already precarious relationship with her mother; and that the production of a live
> baby is the only solution she can find to preserve her emotional balance . . . The
> pregnancy is an attempt to heal. . . . rather than it being a symptom of emotional
> disease, it actually is evidence of attempted emotional recovery. (1956, 3)

The overemphasis on neurotic factors has tended to obscure certain
realities. The fact is—we are no longer living in a Victorian era. The principle of
condoned corruption comes to the surface. Both girls and boys are besieged by
all kinds of erotic allurements—advertisements, popular magazines, and R-
rated movies are all intended to stoke the hormonal urges, yet young people are
expected to refrain from sexual intercourse. A certain cultural contradiction
comes through.

The decade of the 1960s saw a cracking of the overdependence on the
application of psychoanalytic principles. Social workers were exposed to
systems theory, and this provided them with a way to view the phenomenon
from multiple perspectives. Frameworks such as systems theory, family theory,
role theory, and the ideological revolution became, in effect, competing
theories. Bernstein's (1963) claim that social workers had not sufficiently
accepted multiple theories of causation began to be heeded. His exhortation to
give up the stereotyped image of the unmarried mother as an irresponsible
person began to give way to some flexibility in service delivery. By now the
term "birth mother" had replaced "unmarried mother" in the literature and
lexicon in the field.

Role of the Birth Father

In all of this movement and rapidly changing times, the role of the father
was all but ignored. Consistent with the psychological perspective, he was
viewed as a tool for what the girl wanted unconsciously, which was a baby (as a
way of resolving her own personal internal conflicts). A popular view was that
he was an unwitting accomplice whose own personal problems complemented
those of the girl, each of whom sought the other to meet their own individual
needs (Young 1954).

It was a rare experience for an agency worker to provide services to the male
in the picture. Prior to 1972, he was considered, by society and law, to have no
parental rights. Then came the *Stanley vs. Illinois* decision. This landmark case
pitted an unmarried father against the state. Stanley was a man who was living
in a common-law relationship with a woman, fathered her children, and
maintained a semblance of a relationship with his common-law wife. When she
died, the state made the children wards and removed them from Stanley's

custody. He protested on the grounds of violation of his Fourteenth Amendment equal protection rights, claiming that he was dealt with differently because of his marital status. The United States Supreme Court agreed, ruling that the parental rights of an unwed father could not be disregarded. The Court, however, did not spell out those rights. Nevertheless, the decision sent shock waves through adoption agencies in the country, with procedures set up to obtain the father's parental rights' termination as well. (This decision became the basis of a number of battles over custody of the children, including the famous baby Jessica and baby Richard cases.) Today, agencies are much more willing to work with birth fathers, and in many cases, the social worker will provide services to both mother and father.

But what do we really know about birth fathers? Not much, but more than we knew a generation ago when the courts accorded fathers' legal rights. According to a study carried out on 125 birth fathers, he typically: (1) is young, unemployed, and a student; (2) felt unprepared to assume a parental role; and (3) is white, middle class, and Christian (O'Neill 1994).

But the specter of birth fathers (perceived as) as having control over the adoption frequently raises concerns in the birth mothers. In many cases, they are loath to involve the fathers for a variety of reasons: (1) the relationship is over, and they may have some unresolved (hurt) feelings about the father's disappearance from the scene; (2) they may fear that the fathers will prevent the adoption from taking place; and (3) they cannot pretend they don't know the identity of the birth fathers. In fact, if the truth be known, many completed adoptions today are potentially in jeopardy because the birth mother stated *officially* that she didn't know his identity. (I have encountered many a birth mother in my practice who stated that they knew the identity of the birth father but officially they were taking the position of ignorance.)

This is obviously an area in which there is much change. The courts will have to be clearer on the exact nature of birth fathers' rights in the future. The birth father and the agency still engage in an approach-avoidance process, although this is getting better. Many times he anticipates condemnation for his behavior. His own guilt feelings lead him to anticipate punishment; all too often he receives just that—both from our laws and our punitive attitudes. The societal attitude that he is immoral, irresponsible, or just plain bad makes it improbable, if not impossible, to make meaningful contact with him.

This societal attitude reflects itself in a strange quirk in the literature. The adjective "putative" is frequently, if not invariably, used in referring to the birth father. This is really a derogatory reference aimed at the unmarried mother, for it means that he is only suspected, alleged, or reputed to be the father of the baby, suggesting a degree of promiscuity on her part. But in my experience, the vast majority of unmarried mothers are quite aware of the identity of the baby's father. And in light of *Stanley v. Illinois,* it is absolutely essential to identify him and apprise him of the forthcoming legal procedures relative to adoption.

The Birth Mother

By contrast, there is a great deal of information concerning the unwed mother. Most authors agree that she is not a stereotype, but a human being who has been affected by a complex web of dynamics and circumstances, that the only thing she has in common with others in her situation is the carrying of the baby, and that the pregnancy is an obvious problem that cannot be denied and about which a decision has to be made.

Crisis theory allows us to understand the emotional trauma the young woman feels in dealing with her dilemma. The mechanism of denial may be pervasive and work for a while, but prolonged cessation of menses, body changes, and, finally, fetal movement make her realize the full extent of her problem. While in some cases the denial extends throughout the entire pregnancy, this is indeed the rarest of cases. By the fifth month, she typically has to confront the reality of the situation; denial no longer works, and anger over the pregnancy may take its place. She may experience loneliness, despair, and total abandonment. Telling her parents of her plight is one of the most difficult tasks facing her. By the time she comes to see a counselor, a depressive reaction may have set in.

The timeliness of treatment measures offered is another aspect of the process derived from crisis theory. Because the unmarried mother comes for help in a state of crisis and panic precipitated by her pregnancy, she is particularly amenable to measures offered. (Of course, the exacerbating elements of her own mother's anxiety, her father's withdrawal, and her boyfriend's emotional and physical isolation only serve to heighten her own sense of hopelessness.) Studies indicate that the more timely the help proffered, the more immediate and efficacious the results. It is, therefore, vital that her physician recognize the signs of loneliness and despair and be attuned to her psychological needs. While it is undoubtedly easier for the woman to undergo a physical examination than to explore her feelings about the situation, counseling should be considered from the outset. Again, it has been my experience that those who have availed themselves of counseling measures offered, who have dealt with the loss and betrayal issues paramount in the uniqueness of these problems, stand a better chance to "let go" and resume their lives postpartally.

On the other hand, many unmarried mothers choose to forego counseling measures for a variety of reasons. For some, the denial may still be operative, at least regarding their feelings about the anticipatory loss. Such a girl told me, "I just want to get this over with once and for all. I don't want to see the baby, know if it's well, or what sex it is. I just want to be knocked out throughout delivery and pretend it never happened so that I can go on with my life." Another reason for rejecting counseling is because the thought of loss is too painful, emotionally—by not talking about their feelings, the sense of loss is somehow dissipated, or repressed.

However reasonable this attitude is in dealing with the impact of such strong feelings, I consider it unwise. Many women who have done this eventually have to come to terms with their feelings of loss. It may take months or even years, but eventually, these feelings surface. That is why I step out of my neutral role for a moment and suggest they deal with the birth experience in some way (if only to open their eyes for a second). I also recommend, for those who are sure they want to go ahead with placement, that they consider not nursing the baby, as the separation is too overwhelming, and I warn them that leaving the hospital (without the baby) will seem strange since they came in with something but are leaving without it.

The need for the neutrality of the worker's position cannot be overemphasized. Because messages can be so subtly and unconsciously communicated, the worker must know and control his/her own predilections or biases. For both ethical and legal reasons, the girl must be truly free to make the decision regarding placement and consider what it is that she wishes to do. This does not mean that the worker cannot entertain a personal or clinical opinion regarding the best interest of the child, but that he must keep it under control. To do otherwise might unethically influence her judgment and might even be in violation of the "informed consent," thereby jeopardizing the validity of the entire adoption process.

For those who come in requesting adoptive placement, I usually start off with the question, "How difficult do you think the giving up process will be for you?" This gives her a chance to identify her thought processes on a continuum that ranges from "not difficult at all" to "extremely difficult." It also gives the clinician an opportunity to gauge the strength of her ego and learn ways to help the most.

The girl uses a number of psychological mechanisms to protect herself from the overwhelming feelings of attachment and loss. One is rationalization. She tells herself that without her pregnancy, an infertile couple would not have the experience of parenthood. A variation of this theme is that giving up the baby is the decent thing to do, a charitable act of the highest order, and that out of an expression of love for the child, a double grace, as it were, is accomplished; providing a two-parent home for a child and providing a baby for a childless couple. Still another variant of this same theme, particularly for girls with a religious or spiritual bent, is thinking that she is, in a sense, God's instrument for the aforementioned double grace. What makes all of these examples a rationalization is that there is a current of reality in their thinking. Another mechanism used to defend herself from the pain of loss is thinking about the baby, not as her own baby, but as the adoptive couple's baby. This is, essentially, the defense of isolation, wherein the thought is emotionally disconnected from the feeling associated with that thought.

During the critical stages of working through the feelings of anguish, loneliness, fear, and panic, she will frequently encounter disturbing thoughts of one kind or another. Some thoughts about parenting the baby are frightening when she considers that awesome responsibility associated with it. Some thoughts about placing the baby are associated with guilt feelings relative to this decision. In my experience, there is no one set pattern. Literally weeks go by during which time she is absolutely convinced that her decision—whatever it is—is the correct decision for her. In subsequent weeks, the opposite decision will evoke the same reaction of certainty. What is important to remember is that such vacillation is common and crucial to the decision-making process. I refer to such vacillation as "head-heart" responses. The head response is basically an intellectual one. It says: "I am pregnant. I am not in a position to give this child a home and the love he needs, and he is better off placed with a family that can provide him with the love and security he needs." This response is tied to the decision to place, obviously. The heart response is emotional and linked to the decision to keep. It goes as follows: "This is my baby. I have a bond with it, we live off each other and need each other. Nobody has a greater right to this baby than the natural mother, and I am that person." Until the head and heart responses find some means of accommodating each other, confusion reigns, but is dissipated through a supportive therapeutic relationship.

Certain principles to guide the counseling process might be helpful, but one point should be made clear. The professional relationship, as the medium through which help is offered and received, is critical, and has never been accorded the credit it deserves. While the counselor must be clear about his or her own motives in providing guidance, the following principles will prove helpful:

1. Remember that work with a birth mother requires considerable skill. She usually comes to the initial interview with a great deal of anxiety, not really knowing what to expect. It is your job to let her express herself about her situation in an atmosphere that conveys warmth and understanding. In facing the responsibility of impending parenthood, usually without support, she anticipates condemnation.

2. Establish rapport to facilitate communication. Help her feel relaxed and protected. In a way that seems natural to you, show warmth, interest, and understanding of her and her situation.

3. Make efforts to clarify just what you will be doing together. After inquiring what thoughts she has about what she would like to get out of the counseling, I usually tell her what I will not be doing—which is to tell her what to do in relation to the baby. (This helps her relax in her defensiveness in feeling out of control of the situation.) I then tell her what I will be doing —which is to help her think through just what she wants to do, taking into account her feelings about the baby, her parents, the birth father, and significant others.

4. Help her understand that in this crisis situation, she will be barraged by a host of feelings, some of which may be quite new to her. Anger, guilt, hurt, betrayal, and exploitation are only a few examples. The process involves helping her to deal with these feelings in constructive, healthy ways. Without question the feeling of impending loss is the most profound.

5. Of critical importance is your own attitude about premarital pregnancy, having to give up or having been given up. These cannot be disguised and ultimately will get in the way in your work—thus they must be recognized and confronted constructively.

The birth mother's feelings during pregnancy are dependent on a number of factors: attitudes of her own parents, that is, the extent to which the girl feels they truly understand and are supportive; the attitude of the birth father; her age and level of maturity; and the extent to which she is able to distance herself, emotionally, from the biological bond that is occurring within her. I have noted three specific types of feelings that may vary, depending on the circumstances. The first of these is guilt. While she may attempt to rationalize her decision to place the baby for adoption, an underlying feeling of guilt is related to the perception of abandoning her responsibility to the baby. Guilt may also be stirred up in some girls for wishing to keep the baby because, by her decision, the child is being deprived of a waiting, loving, two-parent situation. The second of these feelings is anger—about being in this predicament (the "why me?" response), and the perception, right or wrong, that other people are interested in her only because she has something they want (the baby). Consideration of her as a human being, with wants and needs of her own, are not at all evident to her. The third feeling is an overwhelming sense of loss, particularly if adoption placement is the considered plan. Many young women who leave the hospital experience a grief reaction akin to the death of a child. Almost invariably, the sight of a newborn will elicit a totally unexpected crying spell. At this point, everyone is aware that she is finally in touch with her feelings of loss.

A warm, supportive, nonjudgmental atmosphere will allow the woman to think through her situation and discuss the practical aspects of her planning free from coercion. The counselor who helps the unmarried woman face the thunderous impact of losing a child is responsible for helping her examine her own life as well as the life of her unborn child. This may involve assistance with housing or employment, but most importantly, it involves helping her to identify her strengths and, as she finds satisfaction in making the best decision for herself and the baby, helping her to feel good about herself.

In assisting the woman in decision making, the counselor must help her to separate fact from fantasy, help her to see the realities involved with raising a child alone and with relinquishing a child she may never see again. Although not always successful in this respect, the counselor who genuinely respects the woman and offers sincere help and understanding during this painful time in her life will become an important support system for her.

There have been very few systematic attempts to evaluate the overall effects of the pregnancy and consequent decision making for the unmarried woman. Evidence is increasingly clear, however, that the unmarried mother feels she is completely alone in an insensitive, uncaring world. Recent research recognizes that even prior to relinquishing the child, perhaps as soon as she first experiences fetal movement, she experiences a grief reaction in anticipation of the loss. The denial of pregnancy, which can be equated with the denial stage characteristic of all mourning reactions, may be experienced in conjunction with the feeling of fetal movement, leading to intensely conflicting emotions.

As the delivery date approaches, the anxiety mounts accordingly. The coexisting emotions of attachment and detachment are confusing. Love for the baby, guilt over relinquishing her responsibilities, concern for the baby's future, and loss over what she thinks would be fulfilling experiences of observing the miracle of growth are obviously perceptions of considerable consternation for her.

The flood of emotions can erupt into fits of anger and rage. Usually the girl herself is unaware of her own dependency needs, her needs to be taken care of, and may verbally attack *anyone* with whom she comes into contact.

Renee was seventeen years old, a high-school junior with better than average grades, who learned of her pregnancy during the sixth month. Having been born as an illegitimate child herself, she had strong feelings about the poor care she received at the hands of her mother. In Renee's case, her own plans during the pregnancy were complicated by her mother's demand that Renee find another place to live. After consulting an attorney who agreed to place the baby, Renee was housed by a young couple (not the prospective adoptive parents) who agreed to board Renee as a charitable gesture.

Counseling measures were instituted as a precautionary measure to ensure that all the services Renee might need would be available to her.

During their first two sessions, Renee spoke openly about her view that a child needs a two-parent family, that she was unable to provide it with the nurturing needed, that a child needs more than mere material subsistence, and that she should have been placed herself by her mother rather than her having attempted to become a struggling single-parent family. (It became obvious to the counselor that Renee was viewing the unborn child as an extension of herself, and that she felt she could make the decision she believed her mother ought to have made years ago.)

Just when everything seemed to be going according to schedule, Renee called the counselor to state that she wouldn't need to see him again. When asked why, she launched into a tirade about how she was feeling used throughout this entire process. She enumerated the people whom she felt were getting something out of her pregnancy: the adoptive parents, the doctor, the lawyer, and the counselor. All she was getting was the pain—both physical and psychological—and would have nothing to show for her investment.

At the hospital, Renee continued to exhibit the same pattern of behavior with the hospital social worker. At first she was congenial, expressing the view that she was comfortable with her decision to place the baby. But her irritation mounted with each question of exploring her feelings, and in a rage, she ordered the social worker out of her room. She eventually signed the release but it was obvious to all that the only way in which Renee could surrender her rights to the baby was with a dramatic and histrionic attack on the people whom she was convinced were out to exploit her (author's private practice).

Expressions of anger are not uncommon in response to the range of emotions the woman faces. A grieving period is necessary but one should remember that not everyone does her grief work in the same way. With some it is prolonged, lasting months or even years. With others, the mourning period virtually escapes detection. Of course, many grieve quietly because they were conditioned not to show feelings of hurt, shame, or embarrassment. The important thing to remember, though, is that whether the grieving takes a month or a year, it involves a *process* that cannot be dictated by the intellect or logical reasoning but by the emotional makeup of the individual in question and how she typically and characteristically deals with separation and loss.

One young woman was surprised at her emotional reaction of anger after placement, not realizing its enormous impact on her. "My arms ache because I'll never be able to hold him. My overall feeling is that I feel cheated. I feel cheated because I won't be around to see him cut his first tooth. I feel cheated because I won't be there when he comes home from school. I feel cheated because I won't be there to see him go off to his prom . . . or to see him graduate from high school. I feel cheated because I won't be a part of his life when he gets married."

The decision to place or not to place is a mighty one indeed, and for the first time, the unmarried mother must make the most momentous decision in her young life. Some girls panic and even want others to make that decision for her.

Pamela was sixteen years old and had dropped out of her junior year in high school three weeks before the delivery date. After a normal labor and delivery, she scarcely looked at her newborn son. When she was asked what she wanted to do, she said that she knew she couldn't bring the baby home as her mother was ill and unable to care for the child. Pamela wanted to return to school the following semester. When asked about signing the consent, she balked and asked if the baby could be placed in a foster home while she sorted out her own feelings.

Visitation was irregular but even when she visited, the emotional distance she maintained with the baby was obvious to all. It was apparent that she was attempting to protect herself from any form of maternal attachment.

After four months of very little activity on the case, Pam was asked what her plans were in relation to the baby. She again balked, stating she needed more time. The social worker told her she could have no more than an additional two months, but that some decision would have to be made at that time. She agreed.

The additional two months went by with no visitation and no plan to take the baby home. The agency decided, at that point, that the decision was too weighty for Pamela to handle, and all of her actions seemed to indicate that she wanted the court to decide for her, and that she would abide by the involuntary termination as determined by the court.

This line of thinking was explained logically and carefully to the judge. However, he did not heed the advice of the agency worker, and put the question directly on Pam's shoulders. He said, in effect: "Pamela, this is your baby. Either you take him home or you surrender your rights to him. There is no other option." Pam looked at the surrender papers, her hand trembling, signed them, and bolted out of the courtroom, crying disconsolately. The court had made her face her guilt about not wanting to assume this responsibility (from the author's private practice).

This case illustrates several points about the practice of termination of parental rights and adoption practice:

1. It is considered poor placement practice and, indeed, detrimental to a child's growth and development, to remain in foster care for an extended period of time. In all probability, the six-month waiting period was too long, posing problems of bonding with the eventual adoptive parents.

2. Pamela's immaturity was such that she could not accept the responsibility of making an adult decision.

3. The courts have tended to view an involuntary termination with the gravest of reservations. Taking a legalistic position, the evidence would have to be quite weighty before such action would be deemed justifiable.

Sometimes the birth mother is inundated with feelings that overwhelm and overpower her. Paula was such a person. A twenty-year-old who had been expecting some support from her boyfriend, she finally felt abandoned and angry—and her anger frightened her. In essence, she didn't know if she could contain her anger. My advice was to sit down and write her boyfriend a letter, with no holds barred. Whether she actually sent it to him was something we would decide later. The next day she came in and showed me the following letter:

Donald,
  I hate you so much right now. I'm so angry I want to hurt you. I want to hurt you like you hurt me. I want you to feel the hurt that I'm feeling.
  I think you're a coward. You don't have the maturity or the emotional capability to face this situation like a man. I know you're only 20 years old but . . . so am I. You have no sensitivity because you're afraid.
  I hate you because you got me into this and then you left. You avoided the situation and ran and left me to deal with it. You . . . made me so many empty promises and told me you loved me and that you would be there for me. You're such a . . liar. I don't know how you can even respect yourself or look at yourself in the mirror.
  It's not fair. . . . *I'm* the one who has to carry this baby. *I'm* the one that has to have it and give it up. *YOU?* You don't have to do [anything]. *My* body is changing, *my* emotions are raging, and you couldn't care less. You don't give a [care], and I hate you for that.
  You don't have one stupid mature bone in your body. You have no idea what the word responsibility means. You're so . . . used to having everything handed to you on a silver platter. So you avoid things you don't want to do or deal with. You have no idea what the words love, honesty, loyalty, responsibility,

maturity, support, and understanding mean. You say one thing and then you do another. You're . . . spineless. . . .

I have tried to understand you, and I gave you so many . . . chances—you disappointed me and did nothing but hurt me all summer and I made excuses for you and forgave you. I tried. . . . That's more than you can say. You just gave up and walked away.

You are one big walking disappointment. . . . You're a failure. . . . I wish I'd *never* met you. You never cared about me. You just wanted to get me into bed. You're a living lie. How does it make you feel to know that? You must have *no* conscience whatsoever. I don't know how you live with yourself. You are the poorest excuse for a human I have ever seen.

You are so self-centered. All you think about is me-me-me. All you do is feel sorry for yourself. Get out of your self pity . . . and look around. . . . Look at how good you've got it. You think this is hard for *you?* Try being me for one day. You couldn't do it. You'd never make it. You wouldn't be able to run and avoid if your were me, *then* how would you feel? Trapped, betrayed, cheated, angry? You bet . . . you would. You think you're scared *now?* You don't know . . . about being scared and feeling completely alone. You would never be able to deal with this if you were me. I hope someone hurts you some day as much as you've hurt me. I hope someone disappoints you as much as you've disappointed me. You are one big coward. You're nothing but a failure in my eyes, Donald.

You know, you can run from me and the baby and this situation—but you can't run from yourself. . . . You're probably hurting yourself more than you're hurting me. In that case—justice is served. I'm going to come out of this on top, because I'm *dealing* with it. I deserve so much better than you. I pity the next woman who falls for your phony masks. I got to see the real you and [the] true irresponsible, lying failure that you are. You'll never amount to anything. You'll just spend the rest of your life running from yourself wondering why you can't escape. . . . I *almost* feel sorry for you.

When we began this relationship, I told you that honesty and trust were the most important things in a relationship to me. You shred *any* ounce of trust I had left for you—lies, disappointments, broken promises are what you gave me. At least you're out of my life and can't hurt me anymore. You're gone—I can move on now. I will survive this experience and you'll probably never escape it.

After writing this letter, Paula said she felt much better and was in control again. She chose not to send the letter. But each person reacts differently, and each person learns how to handle feelings in ways that work best for her. She was satisfied that she got these feelings out in the open.

Not all birth mothers let go with the anger and struggle characterized by the previous cases. Some let go with a rational, logical process, the thinking of which is revealed in the following interview:

Q. When you found out you were pregnant, what was your immediate reaction and what was some of your thinking?

A. I guess my first response was "why me?" Why couldn't it have been anybody else in the world but me? Then I started hoping, I guess, that somehow I was wrong—that something else was causing this.

Q. Where about in this pregnancy was it that you knew—your first month?
A. Oh, I knew right away.

Q. You knew right away?
A. I knew after three weeks that I was pregnant. I went to a doctor when I was four-and-a-half months along just to try to convince myself, I guess, that I was wrong.

Q. Well, when you said "why me," that didn't sound like a denial kind of response. It sounded like an anger response. The denial response would have been "not me." Did that come across too?
A. Yes, but I don't remember that one came before the other. They were all kind of bunched up together.

Q. When was it that you were able to tell people—like family?
A. Well, I didn't tell my family until when I went to the doctor, four-and-a-half months later, so I could show them I got help from the doctor, and then I told my parents. And I told the rest of the family and most of my friends and most of my other relatives.

Q. Do you remember the reaction of your family?
A. They handled it a lot better than I thought they would; I would say it was very supportive.

Q. They were concerned about what you were going through. Is that right?
A. Right. In talking to me about my options and whether I have made a decision. I decided right away that I was going to place the child.

Q. Was there wavering in that decision?
A. Not really. In the hospital when I was holding the baby, I came, I guess, as close as I ever did in changing my mind.

With open adoptions, you are dealing with people who know each other. In the previous case (Paula), the adoptive couple seemed to fit in beautifully with the kind of lifestyle Paula wanted for her child. After she delivered at the hospital, however, she called me in a panic, telling me everyone was in her hospital room (the adoptive parents, the social worker from the agency, and the attorney). She was sobbing uncontrollably, but agreed not to sign any papers until I arrived.

I came to the hospital room, asked for some privacy with Paula, and the first thing she told me was that she was feeling so much pressure that she didn't know what to do. We explored her options, helped her separate the facts from her feelings, but I asked her not to give her consent *unless* and *until* she was certain that this was what she wanted.

In recent years, a new approach to practice situations has all but obliterated the medical model, emphasizing pathology of the birth mother, in favor of an empowerment model, emphasizing strengths. This new thrust has been partly due to the changing times and norms, in which birth mothers have the power and control to make choices concerning the children they bear. It is also partly due to a change in ideological perspective of the mental health field in general.

This fairly new orientation is termed a "strengths perspective." It is a shift in focus from seeing people as possessing deficits to seeing people as having strengths, resources, and potentialities to govern their own lives. This strengths perspective has been translated into an empowerment focus. Empowerment of birth mothers involves encouraging them to tap into the strengths they possess, taking into account the nature of their problems and habitual coping mechanisms, their values and goals for themselves, both short and long term, and for their children. This approach transcends the field of adoptions and is long overdue.

Melina and Roszia (1993) approximate such a position in their seminal work. Based on their experiences, they offer a number of scenarios where openness creates a situation that requires some resolution—for example, differences as to what name to give a child. The agency worker can continue to offer a mediating role in such case situations.

In summary, we should remember that birth parents are neither monolithic nor of a single variety. One thing for sure is that they experience a loss they have to deal with, and there is an ever-present concern for what is in the best interest of the child, which is the way things ought to be.

Chapter 12

Child Advocacy:
My Role in the Baby Jessica Case

Let us speak less of the duties of children
and more of their rights. —Rousseau

In chapter 2 of this book, I made reference to my employment with the state of Illinois in the child welfare system of that state. Actually, I launched my professional career in 1958, right after my stint in the United States Army.

I had not chosen child welfare work; it more or less fell into my lap. I was taking a few weeks off from work of any kind when I received a telephone call from Mary Sullivan, at that time regional director for the agency that later became the Illinois Department of Children and Family Services. She convinced me to try my hand as a child welfare worker, which later became a labor of love. My job was to work with children whom the court had declared neglected and dependent. For the most part, these children had been so victimized by their parents or parent figures that permanency planning (although the term was not in vogue at the time) was the goal.

The idea of working for and with children excited me, although I am not sure why. In retrospect, it may have had something to do with a one-time experience of having been abused by my second grade teacher at the Patrick Henry Elementary School. It may also have been a function of being a fantasied survivor of the Holocaust, which 1.5 million children did not survive. At any rate, I saw this job as somewhat of a calling.

One of my first experiences on the job was spending all day in juvenile court. I had learned, while in graduate school, that the state of Illinois was the first in the nation to institute the juvenile court philosophy (in 1899). Thus, it came as quite a shock to me when I witnessed first hand the correctional officers bringing young children over, two by two, from their detention home, in handcuffs! I asked myself, if Illinois is the standard bearer for the rights of children, where does this leave the rest of the country?

I never forgot my child welfare roots and continued to perceive my work in the adoption field as a specialized form of child welfare work. After living in Kentucky for eight years, I was drawn back to Chicago for my doctoral studies; while there, I accepted an appointment to teach at the Indiana University School of Social Work at Indianapolis, where I remain.

I had never thought of myself as a child advocate, but secretly knew I was. I had a good working relationship with the people at the National Council for Adoption, and it was in this connection that my name was given to Robby DeBoer, who called me at home in December 1991 to tell me her plight and ask my assistance.

This phone call brought me in to what was to become one of the most dramatic and publicized legal battles. She told me of their legal custody fight with the Iowa child welfare system. A social worker from California, Annette Baran, had stated in an affidavit that removing Jessica from their home would not prove to be harmful to the youngster. Would I be able to render an opinion that said otherwise? After gathering a few facts about the length of the time they had Jessica, her date of birth, plus learning that this social worker had never seen Jessica or anyone else in the family, I advised Robby that I certainly could offer an alternate view; the literature on attachment and separation is replete with data about the emotional effects of such separations. I was shocked to find out that this expert from California had never seen Jessica and the DeBoers, and I told Robby that before I could testify about the potential effects of removal, I first needed to see the three of them together, evaluate the nature of the bond, and then determine how the separation would most likely affect this nearly one-year-old child.

Facts about the case are as follows:

1. 8 February 1991—Jessica was born to Cara Clausen in Cedar Rapids, Iowa.

2. 10 February 1991—Cara signed release of custody, relinquishing her rights to the child, in the presence of two witnesses. She named Scott Seefeldt as the father, who also signed a release of custody form.

3. 25 February 1991—A termination of parental rights hearing took place in the juvenile court of Linn County, Iowa. Neither she nor the named father

appeared. Had she shown up, she could have revoked her earlier release and probably had the baby returned to her custody. On this same date, petitioners Jan and Roberta DeBoer were named as legal custodians.

4. 6 March 1991—Cara filed request to revoke release of custody order while admitting she lied about the birth father's identity. She then named Daniel Schmidt as the child's father.

5. 27 March 1991—Dan Schmidt filed petition for intervention in adoption proceeding in district court. One month later, blood tests were ordered to determine the biological father, results that were not returned for six months.

6. 24 September 1991—Learning that Dan Schmidt had abandoned two other children, the DeBoers filed petition to terminate Schmidt's parental rights. The trial judge (1) refused to admit evidence of such abandonment; (2) held that Schmidt was the father; (3) dismissed the claim of abandonment; and (4) refused to consider the issue of best interest of the child, ordering change of custody to Schmidt on 27 December 1991.

It was at about this time that arrangements were made to have me interview the DeBoers, assess the bond, and predict the effect of such a separation on Jessica.

Arrangements were made for the DeBoers to visit with me in Indianapolis, and in order to provide a home-like setting for Jessi, I saw them in the family room of my home. My agreement with Robby was that I would evaluate the bond between the three of them together as well as Jessi's relationship with each of them separately. I would then send my evaluation directly to their attorney regardless of the findings, but my main concern would be Jessica and how this change of custody would probably affect her should a peremptory court order require them to surrender her.

The DeBoers arrived on schedule after their five-hour drive from Ann Arbor to Indianapolis. I found Jessi to be a wide-eyed, inquisitive youngster who warmed up to me after about fifteen minutes.

It was the spontaneity in the chemistry between Jessi and each of her parents that impressed me. When one parent left the room, she was just as comfortable with the other parent, and when they spoke to her, she was able to track the message. Of this visit, which lasted a good three hours, Robby wrote (1994):

> We liked Dr. Smith right away, because of the way he interacted with Jessi. We could see that he really understood children. He got down on the floor with her to play, and let her lead him in their games. . . . He would clap for her, and Jessi would smile at him and clap for herself. . . . It was a day well spent. (89)

I told the DeBoers that I was very satisfied with the bond, that I could see how attached she was to them, and that, given her age and stage of development, separating from them would be quite difficult, even traumatic for her. But I also reassured them that because of the foundation of security they had given her, she would eventually recover.

The next day, I sent my affidavit to the Iowa attorney. It read, in part:

> The bonding and attachment issue is central in this case. Bonding and attachment refers to the reciprocal feelings between parent and infant, most stereotypically between mother and infant, but one which includes the father as well. It is a phenomenon that transcends the adoptive or nonadoptive status of the family. Adoptive parents do bond with their children as do biological parents. In a study by Singer and his associates, no differences were found between adoptive and nonadoptive mothers relative to attachment. Further, many theorists and developmental researchers have commented on the effects of the precipitous break of this bond, particularly the works of John Bowlby, Rene Spitz, and Mary Ainsworth. Cumulative clinical experience has demonstrated conclusively that a child needs a reliable, ongoing attachment to a primary caregiver, and that the child suffers grievously, if not irreparably, if that attachment is interrupted.
>
> When a parental role is well carried out, whether biological or adoptive, the state of "psychological parenthood" is reached. This notion is a constant reference guide for the courts in dealing simultaneously with psychiatric and legal issues. It is developed, theoretically, in the bestseller, *Beyond the Best Interests of the Child* by Goldstein, Freud, and Solnit. State these authors:
>
> The physical realities of his conception and birth are not the direct cause of his emotional attachment. This attachment results from day-to-day attention to his needs of physical care, nourishment, comfort, affection, and stimulation. Only a parent who provides for these needs will build a psychological relationship to the child on the basis of the biological one and will become his psychological parent in whose care the child can feel valued and wanted. An absent biological parent will remain, or tend to become, a stranger.
>
> The tasks of Jan and Roberta DeBoer have been to become Jessica's psychological parents, and to develop a sense of entitlement (feelings of rightfulness to the child). Out of my need to assess this phenomenon, I conducted a clinical interview with the DeBoers, where I could observe firsthand the nature of the relationship between these adults and the infant in question.
>
> The results of my three-hour interview with the DeBoers indicated the unequivocal existence of such a parental bond. Jessica smiled and cooed, as one would expect of an eleven-month-old, and it is quite obvious that she has developed trust and a willingness to engage with people. She stands without support, and claps her hands with delight when she accomplishes a motor task she previously had not mastered. On the issue of entitlement, Jan and Roberta DeBoer feel this is their child, and their anxiety over the tenuousness of their situation has not diminished the quality of this bond with Jessica.
>
> There has been much discussion on the subject of emotional disturbance among adoptees. These assertions are (virtually exclusively) made by clinicians

who see disturbed families all day long and do not appreciate or value the methodological research issues involved. (*The Adoption Triangle*, for example, is not a book about adoption, but about a group of individuals who sought out their birth families. It is, by most accounts, a biased sample, the findings of which do not, in any way represent adoptive families across the board). Dr. Alfred Kadushin of the University of Wisconsin amassed studies of adoption outcome in various parts of the world. Of over 2,600 placements, 84 percent were found to be in the successful range, giving clear evidence that adoption is an eminently successful venture.

It is my view that a strong parental bond exists between Jessica and each of her (psychological) parents. This child, who has never laid eyes on the putative father, basically has no relationship with that person. To remove Jessica from the only security she has ever known to a situation fraught with psychological dangers would be most detrimental to her continued well-being. Whatever the reasons for the move, the child will view this event as tantamount to abandonment, complete with feelings of loss, worthlessness, and insignificance. She may become depressed, suffer eating and sleeping disorders, and harbor a resentment over events she cannot understand. In short, the experience may leave her with emotional scars from which she may never recover.

I heard nothing more about the case until the latter part of 1992. My contacts at the National Council for Adoption believed that the court was swayed by the arguments attesting to the potential harm to Jessica's mental health through a precipitous removal. But in reality, wheels were in motion to jeopardize the security of the placement. An appeal on the part of the DeBoers to overturn the district court order was denied. At about the same time, the DeBoers set in motion a request to have the Michigan court decide on the best-interest issue. The judge in the case believed that there was justification in such a request and therefore granted it. That set the stage for the DeBoers's attorney, Suellyn Scarnecchia, to contact me to reevaluate the bond and attend the hearing set for 29 January 1993. I agreed to both of these requests.

I met with Jessica and her parents in the office of the University of Michigan's Child Advocacy Center, using Suellyn's office. Jessica had grown and matured, as one would expect, and her vocabulary had expanded exponentially. The bond I previously noted was even stronger. Jessi continued to enjoy her individual relationship with each parent separately as well as collectively.

But because by now this become a national news story, I decided to appraise Jessi's ability to accept any sort of separation from the DeBoers. I set up an experiment in which I asked both parents to leave the room together, with Jessi staying with me. The instructions were for them to tell her they were leaving but would be right back, and that she could trust me. My worst fears were confirmed in the blink of an eye. Jessi became distraught, hysterical, displaying clinging behavior, and I immediately halted the experiment. My instincts told me that Jessica sensed that something was up to threaten her security, even though she could not verbalize these fears. Nevertheless, I could see that the many times she was in front of the cameras plus the nonverbal fears she saw in the faces of her parents had the cumulative effect of eroding the security she once felt.

I'll never forget the look of horror in her face. I knew that I would see this look again if Jessi were ever taken from the DeBoers. And with the rancorous feelings that existed between the two sets of parents, I couldn't imagine an amicable transfer taking place. Make no mistake, Jessica knew something was up, even though she couldn't say what.

I had a unique role in the proceedings. While each side was able to call in their experts, my role was that of an evaluator of the bond and the quality of parenting each set would offer. I was to have interviewed Dan and Cara on Saturday, 30 January at 9:30 A.M., and in fact, had my questions laid out to evaluate how realistic or unrealistic they were about her coping mechanisms. At 9:23, a call came in to Suellyn's office, advising us that they chose not to appear. I was personally disappointed because I saw this as an opportunity to know them as people and potential parents, as well as to quell their concerns, fears, or apprehensions that I viewed them as adversaries; nothing could be farther from the truth.

The hearing on Friday, as I recall, commenced with some of the expert testimony. The presence of David Brodzinsky lent a certain credibility to the proceedings; he is an internationally acclaimed researcher. He spoke from the vantage point of the adoptive experience, reminding the court that he had never met the DeBoers or Jessica. He stated rather clearly that adoptive mothers do bond with children and that taking a two-year-old who had bonded out of her surroundings was fraught with difficulty. He also cautioned against changing her first name, as reports were circulating that the Schmidt's planned to do (and, in fact, this did occur). Vicki Bennett, a clinical social worker in Ann Arbor, who may have seen Jessica, also testified about the harmful effects of separation.

My turn was on Monday morning, 1 February. I was on the stand for three hours, explaining what Jessica's needs were, from my perspective. I did my best to keep the focus on Jessi, what she needed, and how she would, in my judgment, react to a sudden transfer (based on my experiment). The attorney for the Schmidts, Marian Faupel, did her best to discredit my testimony, at times asking such personal questions that even Judge Ager questioned her as to their purpose. I realized, however, that he was trying to give Ms. Faupel as much latitude as possible. But I could not understand why he allowed her to ask me my age, as if that had any bearing on the issue. She even implied that the Schmidt's not showing up for their interview was my doing (since I wasn't there for the telephone call), which I suppose is analogous to the question of what was Pearl Harbor doing out in the Pacific.

But I held firm to my position that Jessi should remain with the DeBoers, with the Schmidt's gradually assuming a co-parenting role through visitations.

The thrust of my testimony, however, was to inform the court of the nature of Jessica's world (to a not quite two-year-old child) and what separation would mean to her, given the nature of her bond with the DeBoers and where she was in her psychological development. Thus, I stated the following:

> Jessica's perception of the world is one that is providing her with some security and some happiness. At this point in her life, she is *very, very* dependent on these people (the DeBoers) to continue to provide her with that world—and it's a good world. If she were suddenly removed from this secure family life—for whatever reason—that perception would dramatically be altered. She would be inundated with feelings of confusion and betrayal, asking "What is going on with my life? I don't understand this, and I don't understand why you aren't able to keep me. I know you love me and I can't understand this event in my life, which turns my entire world upside down." While those precise words were not in her vocabulary, the feelings are there, which would have profound implications for the rest of her life.

Throughout all of the testimony, the guardians ad litem, who were designated to represent Jessi's best interests, took copious notes. While I was not there throughout the case proceedings, it is my understanding that each one recommended that custody remain with Jan and Robby.

To no one's surprise, Judge Ager ruled in favor of the DeBoers, but they lost on appeal. The higher courts looked at the matter not in terms of the child's needs, but in terms of the constitutional rights of Dan Schmidt, and since he never voluntarily terminated his rights, she belonged to him.

I personally anguished over the decision to return Jessi (a questionable word, since they never had her in the first place) to the Schmidts. There were sleepless nights, and I viewed the date of 2 August (the day she was to be turned over to the Schmidts) as a form of date of execution. The look of anguish on Jessi's face was the same look I had seen on her face in Suellyn's office.

The public outrage over what happened to this little girl was unprecedented, and even lawyers, who understand the legal system better than I do, are at a loss to explain this tragedy. Many feel, in retrospect, that the DeBoers should have turned Jessi over in the beginning of the litigation; by prolonging it, they just made life more complicated for her. They also fault the legal system for allowing this case to drag on in the courts. But the case did underscore the biological bias of the system and relegate the rights of children to a secondary position.

To add to the trauma of losing the only parents to whom she was attached, Jessica was denied a major piece of her own identity—her name. I was appalled by this decision as it only exacerbated her already aggravated sense of loss. Any person who saw the look of terror and anguish on Jessica's face on 2 August must have wondered what happened to our concept of "justice" as it pertains to children. To answer this question, we must address the values involved. Our values hinge on our cognitive understanding of what ought to be, and they underlie our laws, policies, and practice.

Value Issues

The value issues are central to any consideration of laws or policy from which they emanate.

The first such value issue is that parents and children belong together. That is an inviolate law that ranks up there with the Ten Commandments. The biological parent-child relationship is viewed as the most binding and sacrosanct of all relationships. Because this value is so deeply felt by society and courts of law, judges have been loath to remove children from their parents in circumstances of proven and confirmed abuse, except in the most extreme of cases. But the law can and does step in and remove children when it has to, under the power and sanction of *parens patriae* (as the ultimate parent of each child).

The second value issue is that birth parents' rights prevail unless one can conclusively demonstrate that harm will befall a child by forcing him/her to remain with a biological mother or father. When it came right down to it, Dan Schmidt's rights as a father to Jessica took precedence over her rights and needs. His parental history with his other two children was deemed irrelevant. As Charlotte Allen stated, "the greatest revolution in adoption law—and the one with the most implications for Jessica's case—was the recognition that if unwed mothers had a right to veto an adoption, so did unwed fathers" (1993).

Third, since Jessi's needs were never taken into consideration, it necessarily begs the question: What are our children really worth? If a man who has already demonstrated a lack of parenting skills is considered to have more rights than a child begging for some semblance of security in her life, what have we come to in our society?

It is this very basic value issue that impels me to make my most irrepressible observation. The case of Jessica DeBoer is a case of institutionally sanctioned child abuse. This is not to make invidious comparisons between the DeBoers and the Schmidts, but it is to say that by forcibly removing her from the only security she has ever known, the entire court system collapsed on her, leaving her in a state of the highest vulnerability and inability to protect herself. In a word or two, the way our court system is set up, those who are in the greatest risk category are in an emotional straitjacket. It saddens me no end that children continue to be treated as possessions, and that this country values sperm donors' rights as superior to those of helpless children. After all is said and done about the best interest of children, it means nothing when bioparental rights dominate, and this situation must *change* if the concept of "justice" is to apply to children.

I wish to make one other point. It has to do with the casting of blame. I think it is generally understood that whatever could have gone wrong in this case did, in fact, go wrong. Some blame the case failure on the fact that professionals were not involved in the case from the beginning. Michigan is one of those states that prohibits nonagency placements. Thus, the DeBoers went to the state of Iowa to obtain custody. In an article published by the organization of professional social workers, the suggestion is made that an agency service would have provided the child with greater protection (Landers 1993). Interestingly, no mention is made of the misidentification of the biological father by Cara. But naming the wrong man as father could easily have occurred in an agency placement. Thus, I consider that argument a moot point.

What Should Have Occurred in This Case

The tragedy of the baby Jessica case is that the trauma of removing Jessica from one world to another could have been greatly reduced. I see three possibilities, although it is impossible to know how the outcome would have differed if one or all of these suggestions were followed.

1. The DeBoers should have been counseled in the very beginning about the risks involved in this situation (once they were informed about the birth father problems). They may have been, but I am not privy to such information. Neither was Suellyn Scarnecchia (personal communication March 1996).

2. Cara needed grief counseling in the worst way. Since she waived her right to appear at the juvenile court hearing on 25 February 1991, the law assumed her resolution of the conflict (to place or parent the child). It was when she realized the ramifications of this inaction that her grief reached its most acute phase. It was soon after this point that Cara attended a meeting of Concerned United Birth parents, an antiadoption support group for birth parents.

3. Efforts should have been made to appoint a mediator to work with the parents on both sides, working towards the goal of a co-parenting arrangement. Had the focus stayed on Jessi's personal welfare, she could have accommodated this sort of a change in her life provided all parties played by the set-up rules. The trauma of loss for Jessi would then have been

greatly minimized, if not eliminated altogether. But the way the courts set the "resolution," there had to be a winner and a loser, and the way the court system handled it, the biggest loser of all was Jessica.

But there is a movement afoot to make the public aware of the rights and needs of children. Right after the public outcry for reform, an organization sprang up in the Ann Arbor area, with chapters all across the nation, focusing on the need to recognize and deal with the rights of children. It was called the "DeBoer Committee on Children's Rights" and later changed its name to "Hear My Voice."

I have been asked many times if I know how Jessica is faring, and I frankly have to plead ignorance. I have heard reports of the semblance of adjustment, but I am dubious about claims that she is a happy, well-adjusted little girl. Frankly, I am more concerned about her long-term adjustment. I fear that her trust in humanity took a mighty big blow, and that this experience has made her wary and cautious about the permanence of human relationships. I also have the feeling that some day in the future, she will seek out the DeBoers, not knowing that by finding them, she can fill the hole made in her psyche by this tragic experience.

In the future, I trust that children's rights will be given the priority it deserves on the national agenda, that we will agree with Rousseau about giving children their rights, and that we will agree with former Supreme Court Justice Harry Blackmun who called this case one that "touches the raw nerve of life's relationship." In the years to come, I predict that the name of "Jessica DeBoer" will serve as a beacon to light the way for other children's rights and needs, which are being ignored in our present system of justice.

Chapter 13

A Closing Note

Much has been said about the difficulties in the adoptive parenting role. The literature on the subject abounds with references to competing with phantom figures, dealing belatedly with the various forms of narcissistic wounds, and covering up basic feelings of emptiness with a host of self-reassuring messages about one's own worthiness in being selected to parent a given child. Unfortunately, many of these tasks are, in reality, as they have been presented— difficult at best, impossible at worst. Yet most adoptive parents would tell you that these tasks are overplayed and that parenting a child one adopts is essentially no different than any other form of parenting and that the joys and hazards of parenting transcend the adoption issue. In most adoptive families, adoption surfaces on rare occasions, usually in response to a remark made by a neighbor about who the child looks like or in response to a made-for-TV movie with an adoption theme (such as a teenage girl searching out her birth parents). While these situations do occur, and in some cases with a good deal of regularity, it has been my experience that they are rare in most families that have dealt effectively with their feelings about adoption.

Over time, I have noticed an increasing willingness on the part of parents to discuss adoption with their children with overtones of pleasure and positive parenting; however, this was not always, or even primarily, the case as adoption was practiced in the early 1960s. At that time we had many babies to place, and standards were greatly relaxed to accommodate the number of infants that were available for adoption. In those days, the stigma associated with illegitimacy and the humiliation surrounding the circumstances of the conception heightened people's sensitivities to the adoption issue. It was not an unusual occurrence at that time to provide the adoptive parents with background information on the child, only to have many of these parents state that they were not interested in such information. One has to wonder how they handled the child's need for information of his genetic past during the child's developmental milestones. Another development is the tendency to dilute the anonymity associated with the adoption and sealed record process. Certainly, the media has exploited many adoptees' need to find birth parents as well as birth parents' need to find children they gave up years ago. States are becoming more responsive to such requests, aided by the various search groups and organizations, and legislatures are progressively setting up voluntary registers where various parties in the adoption triangle find each other if there is mutual consent. Then the "open adoption" concept can obliterate the anonymity previously afforded, and this practice can have far-reaching effects for adoptive parents and children alike. This practice is currently being evaluated.

I believe that the unique task in adoptive parenthood is the development of the feeling that the child really belongs to them. This phenomenon has been referred to as "entitlement." The sense of entitlement, or belongingness, if you will, refers not only to the perception that the child really belongs to them but also that he or she belongs to them unconditionally and even exclusively. Now, this is a relatively easy procedure when one has a biological child, and the sense of entitlement for a biological parent probably occurs at an unconscious level. But for adoptive parents, the entitlement is a bit more complicated.

The building blocks of successful adoption are communication, acceptance, and a strong, secure sense of identity. In a close, nurturing family, these factors emerge together. Communication is perhaps the most important, because open communication is necessary for the development of both acceptance and a sense of identity.

Parents who are able to discuss adoption in a direct, honest manner teach their children that adoption is acceptable. It is not necessary and, in fact, it is undesirable that all family communication revolve around adoption. The subject should be neither be dwelled upon nor totally avoided. There is a comfortable middle ground where adoption is acknowledged as a fact and discussed when it is appropriate. When the parent continually brings up the adoption in unrelated conversation, the parent is likely suffering from unresolved anxieties and will communicate these feelings to the child. The parent who purposely avoids discussing adoption often harbors unresolved conflicts as well and may unknowingly send his child the message that adoption is unacceptable. Too much or too little communication regarding the adoption may cause the child to question his own desirability and jeopardize his/her rightful place within the family unit.

The adopted child and his/her parents will have feelings about adoption. The child will likely voice fears and concerns and ask questions about his/her adoption from an early age. Parents who acknowledge and accept their child's feelings put their child on the road to developing a healthy self-identity. Parents who answer their child's questions in a direct, sincere, and loving manner teach the child to accept himself and his place in the family situation.

The ease with which the child accepts his adoptedness is directly related to the degree of success the adoptive parents have had in accepting their own status as adoptive parents. Thus, it is imperative for them to accept their new parenting roles and develop a sense of entitlement to the child if the child is to grow up feeling good about himself.

The parents' feelings about infertility can affect acceptance of the child. Hostility can replace love toward the child if the child is continually viewed as a symbol of biological inadequacy. Open communication between the couple and professional counseling may help resolve feelings about inadequacy. Such counseling toward resolution of problems associated with infertility should take place prior to the adoption of the child whenever possible. Those who come to the realization that sexual capacity must not be equated with producing a child can find great emotional satisfaction in their relationship and in the contribution they can make to a child's growth and development through adoptive parenthood.

A child who experiences honest, open communication and feels that his parents accept him becomes an integral part of the family unit. The child feels that he belongs and identifies him/herself with the family. The "telling" is important to the child's sense of identity. The adoptive parent who assures his child that "you are mine despite the fact that someone else gave birth to you" tells the child that s/he belongs to his/her adoptive family. The child who is taught that adoption is good feels that s/he, too, is good. S/he comes to like him/herself and feels that s/he is a worthwhile and valuable part of the family. The child comes to see that those who care for and love him/her are, indeed, his/her parents.

While adoptees do often encounter difficulties developing a sense of self-identity and resolving the issue of rejection by their birth parents, so do other children, and these factors by themselves may not put adoptees at greater developmental risk than children living with their biological parents. Vastly more important to the growing child is the quality of family life in which he finds himself.

Problems are facts of life in even the most loving, accepting families. Families do not always function in harmonious accord. Friction between family members, particularly between children and their parents, must be anticipated and accepted as natural occurrences. Problems should not be avoided as if they could not or should not exist. For adoptive parents, it may be tempting to attribute parent-child conflict or a child's delayed or inappropriate social behavior to the adoption itself. It is extremely important, and also reassuring, to realize that the most common source of problems are developmental changes that follow a child from infancy to adulthood, not the fact that the child was adopted.

Adoption practice is truly in a state of flux. Stock answers we gave to our children for many decades under the banner of confidential placements no longer seem appropriate. If there is a rule to be followed in imparting information about background, it should be to provide as much information as you can obtain. Gone are the days when secrecy dominated the family scene. That is as it should be; the child has a right to this information. It is part of him/her. In the mediated adoption, the agency worker can be a conduit for continuing information of a medical or psychiatric nature. With fully disclosed adoptions, each party must uphold the agreement made with each other. Few things in life can be more devastating than a birth parent who fails to show up when the child expects a visit. Derogatory remarks made about the birth parents serve to undermine the identity issues for a child. And these issues are both complex and monumental. Because research on openness is still in the embryonic stage, no one can predict with any degree of certainty what the future holds in adoption practice.

There are comparable themes of loss for all parties associated with adoption. For birth parents, the major issue is the loss of a child and lack of information about his/her subsequent development. For the adoptive parent, the experience of fantasied loss related to reproduction is painful and needs sensitive attending to by the spouse and/or professionals. For the adoptee, the loss of birth parents and feelings of rejection may be exacerbated if sufficient background information is not provided.

On the issue of the search, I recommend an honest, open approach that will allow the adoptee to consider the multitude of factors he/she must consider and to allow the final decision to rest with the child. Parents must be careful not to impose their own views in either direction. A comment such as "after all we have done for you, you want to seek out your birth parents" is really unproductive. Likewise, a comment like "I don't blame you for wanting to seek out your birth parents—if I were adopted, I would want to seek them out" doesn't give the child much of an opportunity to make the choice himself or herself. If it truly is a decision to be made by the adoptee, the parents must not impose their own views. That is why I strongly urge adoptive parents to first know their own feelings on the subject.

The study undertaken to examine the attitudes on openness in adoptions revealed some interesting findings. For one thing, it revealed a higher degree of acceptance than previously thought. The study shed some light on an area that has thus far had very little systematic research. It does appear as if open situations work best when the different roles of birth and adoptive parents are clear and unequivocal. And it does appear as if semiopen may yet prove to be the most preferred of all the alternatives. But the research points out that findings thus far are tentative and calls for continuation of broad-based longitudinal research.

Finally, adoptive parents need to develop an ideological stance that will aid them in setting up a family framework that is both functional and provides gratification for all family members involved. It is offered in the form of a contract, not in a legal sense, but a contract of understanding of the mutuality of roles between parents and children. It recognizes both the similarities and differences between adoptive and biological parenthood.

We are your parents, and, as such, we have certain rights as well as responsibilities. We have the right to care for you and guide you through your youth as we see it. We have the responsibility to care for you, feed and clothe you, nurture you through good and bad times, times when you are healthy s well as times when you are ill or ailing. We recognize that rights and responsibilities are two sides of the same coin and that you cannot have one without the other.

This role did not come "naturally" to us, however. It is a role we requested, hoped for, and even yearned to assume. We petitioned to be given the opportunity to have a child to love and to witness the miracle of growth. We are your parents through a legal process. Before we could rightly call you our own, we had to satisfy the courts that we were qualified to become your parents. That process distinguishes adoptive parenthood from biological parenthood.

It is different in a number of other respects as well. It is different because the law says it's different, as we are required to prove our fitness as parents to the social worker visiting our home. Further, it is different because people are constantly reminding us of your biological parents, remarks such as "isn't he lucky to have people like you to care for him!" or "now maybe you'll have one of your own!" It is different because we know there are other people out there somewhere who are directly responsible for your birth. We feel something for them, most likely, gratitude.

We feel an obligation to work through our own vulnerabilities that these situations create for us because we want to be the best possible parents. This means not adopting you until we are ready—until we have resolved our feelings about not giving birth to you, and coming to grips with our motives for adopting you. We know it would be wrong, for example, to adopt you just because certain children need homes or to make the adoption a "social cause" for which decent people do make sacrifices. We should only adopt because we want to share our love, wanting nothing more in return than what you are able to give.

Sometimes we would like to forget these differences exist and think of you exclusively as our own (which legally you are), but other times we beam with pride over the fact that we adopted you or, more accurately, that we adopted each other. Our love for you has grown and deepened with each passing day, and that is what real love is all about.

Your becoming a member of our family gives you all of the same rights, privileges, and responsibilities as if you had been our biological child. We willingly assume the responsibilities for nurturing your growth and teaching you what is right and wrong in accordance with our own set of values and standards of behavior. We will set limits that we believe you will need in life, regardless of the unpopularity of that decision at that particular time.

Above all, we owe you an open and honest relationship. We will tell you the truth about your beginnings, how you came to us, and what we know about your genetic past. We feel you are entitled to this information. We will give it you to satisfy your curiosity about your biological heritage. We realize that your identity is a composite of both your biological and adoptive heritage and that questions about both aspects of your life are both natural and normal. We always want you to be inquisitive about your beginnings and to take pride in your heritage. Your valuing yourself is as important as our valuing you. Your worth as a person knows no bounds.

Families that are formed by way of adoption face many hurdles as parents carry out their roles. They confront the heredity/environment dilemma at various crossroads. Adoptive parents would like to think the environment is a much weightier factor in the development of their children, but recent evidence shows more and more the influence of heredity. Some feel that there is a choice to be made—an either/or situation. It is a fruitless argument. The fact of the matter is that heredity and environment can only be defined in relation to each other. There can be no heredity without environment: heredity sets limits to the developmental potential of personality, but social experience gives it its concrete form. At birth the infant is not a tabula rasa. There are significant hereditary differences between one infant and the next. Infants vary in personality type, physical type, intellectual development, temperament, motor activity, and so on. Nonetheless, the influence of the environment is immeasurably great in molding the ways our children learn to love and work.

I would like to conclude this work on a personal note. My message is this—adoption is for children. It is a way we come together to form a family and to share the bond that exists therein. In the thirty years my wife and I have been adoptive and biological parents, we have experienced untold joys through love and sharing the beauty of life with each other.

Appendix

Adoption Research Questionnaire

Number_____

<u>Questionnaire</u>

<u>Instructions</u>

This study is designed to determine the nature of attitudes toward some current agency adoption practices. What you are being asked to do is to answer these questions as completely as possible, indicating your thoughts <u>and</u> your feelings about the particular matter. Please remember that there are no right or wrong answers—it is your gut-level response that will be the most helpful.

<u>Part 1</u>

Sex /___/ Female   /___/ Male

Race /___/ Caucasian   /___/ Asian

     /___/ Black   /___/ Other (specify) _____

     /___/ Hispanic

Age _____

Religious Identity (i.e., what do you consider yourself to be?)

/___/ Catholic   /___/ Protestant (which denomination?)

_____

/___/ Jewish   /___/ Other (specify) _____

_____

Occupation or profession _____

Educational background (indicate highest degree earned or last year in school

_____

Are you an adopted person?   /___/ Yes   /___/ No

At the present time, do you have children?   /___/ Yes   /___/ No

If "yes," how many, and are they adopted or biological? _____

Gross family income (round off to closest $1,000) _____

Part 2

This section of the questionnaire is designed to measure your attitudes about certain aspects of adoption practice. Indicate the extent of your agreement with each statement according to the following:

1 = Strongly Disagree
2 = Disagree
3 = Neutral
4 = Agree
5 = Strongly Agree

1. ___ I am confident that the agency will place a child with us within the expected time frame discussed with us.

2. ___ I am confident that the child placed with us will have characteristics and background that match our own.

3. ___ I anticipate that we (my spouse and I) may need to modify our attitudes about the conditions under which the placement will be made (e.g., meeting with the birth parents.)

4. ___ I would be willing to meet with one or both of the birth parents one time prior to the placement.

5. ___ I would feel comfortable with meeting with one or both of the birth parents.

6. ___ I would want to meet with one or both of the birth parents whether or not the agency worker suggested it.

7. ___ An adoptee should have the right of access to all information about his/her birth parents, including their identities.

8. ___ Adopted children should be able to obtain sufficient background information about their genetic origins, but not actual identities of birth parents.

9. ___ It is not necessary to give children background information about their birth families.

10. ___ I think sharing of identities does not interfere with being good adoptive parents.

11. ___ A child should be told of his adoption by the time s/he is four years old.

12. ___ Bringing a child up that one adopts is no different than bringing up a biological child.

Part 3

As a variation of the preceding, the following questions are designed to determine your attitudes about the telling process. Please answer the following in the same way as the previous group of questions.

1. ___ Adopted children should be told about their adoption.

2. ___ Adopted children should be given the circumstances about their conception, if known.

3. ___ Adopted children should <u>not</u> be told that their conception was the result of a rape, if that was the circumstance.

4. ___ Adopted children should be told that their conception was a result of incest, if that was the circumstance.

5. ___ I look forward to telling my (adopted) child about the fact of his/her adoption.

6. ___ I am fearful of telling my (adopted) child about the fact of his/her adoption.

7. ___ I have a fearful fantasy that the day will come when my child's birth parents will intervene in our lives.

8. ___ It makes me anxious to think that, after we have adopted, well-meaning people (relatives, neighbors) will ask us personal, intrusive questions about our child's ancestry.

9. ___ I wonder if I will be as good a mother (father) as this child deserves.

10. ___ It will bother me if my child comes to me and asks what the word "illegitimacy" means.

11. ___ It is a good idea to tell my child that s/he was placed for adoption out of the birth parents' love for her/him.

Part 4

Agencies across the country are experimenting with various forms of openness in adoption. Currently there are three main forms of adoption practice. A brief description of each follows.

Definitions of Adoption Styles - based on DEGREE AND KIND OF POST-PLACEMENT CONTACT between birth- and adoptive families.

1. Closed/Confidential—minimal exchange of biographical/personal information on adoptive parents and birth parents at placement *AND* either no contact between the parties after placement *OR* the exchange of nonidentifying information within the first year (one or two pictures, a letter/update provided for birth parents.)

2. Semi-Open (CONTINUED: NONIDENTIFYING)—active sharing of nonidentifying information (letters, pictures, gifts) that is mediated by the agency. Includes face-to-face meetings as long as parties share only nonidentifying info.

3. Fully-Disclosed (CONTINUED: IDENTIFYING)—sharing of identifying information (last names, addresses, phone numbers) AND direct communication between parties. Often includes ongoing face-to-face contact.

    1. ___ Place an "x" at the one of these practices you prefer.
    2. ___ Place an "xx" at the one practice you least prefer.

The agency advises you that your responses to the previous question is the basis of the length of time it will take to place. You (choose one of the following):

___a. hold firm to your response

___b. revise it to shorten length of time

___c. try to negotiate some form of compromise

___d. other (explain. _____

_____

_____

What do you consider to be the advantages and disadvantages of each of these approaches? You may approach this from the vantage point of the adoptive parents, the child, and/or the birth parents.

	Advantages	Disadvant:
Closed Confidential		
Semi-open		
Fully disclosed/ Open		

All things being equal (i.e., if you had total control of the adoptive situation, and the agency would place a child with you according to your desires on a given date, with no restrictions or strings attached), what is the type of adoption you would opt for? What is/are your reason(s) for your response?

Part 5

The following are analogues or vignettes of adoption situations. Please answer these as if you were in the actual situation.

Analogue #1

You receive a telephone call from a woman who has been searching for the son she gave up for adoption. She believes your son is her biological child, and she has very strong evidence to back up this assertion. She asks to (1) meet with you and (2) to see the child. What would your reaction be to this situation?

____a. refuse to see her

____b. grant her requests as stated

___c. agree to meet with her but not allow her to see your child

___d. ask for some time to consider her request

___e. other (explain) _____ __

_____

_____

Analogue #2

Your nineteen-year-old adopted daughter has, with your knowledge, been attempting to locate her birth parents. She has been successful in locating her birth father and leaves for her first meeting with him in a state of anticipation. She returns sad and dejected. She informs you that she found out that her conception was the result of a one-time only date, a "thank you for a Friday night pizza date." How would you respond? (More than one response is acceptable).

___ a. advise her not to see her father anymore

___ b. attempt to draw out her feelings

___ c. ask her to go for counseling

___ d. take her shopping to cheer her up

___ e. other (explain) _____

_____

_____

Analogue #3

Six months ago you told your eight-year-old son that he is adopted. Ever since then, when you discipline him, he makes remarks such as, "My real mommy wouldn't treat me like this." You have tried to tell him that you are his mommy, and you love him, but he just pulls away from you and goes to his room. How would you respond to this situation?

____ a. keep trying to reassure him

____ b. ignore what he says and hope this behavior will pass

____ c. be especially affectionate

____ d. spend more time with him

____ e. get angry

____ f. other (explain) _____

Your thinking about this situation is as follows:

____ a. I must not allow him to do this to me

____ b. I can't be mad at him because this type of behavior "goes with the adoption territory"

____ c. When he says things like that, it makes me feel inferior as a parent

____ d. "the little ingrate"

____ e. other (explain) _____

Analogue #4

Your fifteen-year-old adopted daughter received a concussion from a fall at the skating rink. Within six months time she began having petit mal seizures. You are interested in finding out if there is any history of epilepsy in her biological ancestry. You only have medical information about the parents, and very sketchy information at that, and the agency that handled the adoption is no longer in business. You know it would be possible to contact the birth mother for additional medical information. What would you do?

____ a. make the contact

____ b. not make the contact

____ c. seek advice from a neurologist

____ d. secure an advocate who would maintain confidentiality

____ e. contact the court

____ f. other (explain) _____

Analogue #5

You and your husband have applied for adoption at the local agency. After five years of waiting the call comes—a baby boy two days old and perfectly healthy. There is just one stipulation. The birth mother insists that she be given the legal right to see the child once a year on his birthday until he is eighteen. What would you do?

____ a. agree to the yearly visitation

____ b. not take the child

____ c. plead with the mother to change her mind

____ d. seek the advice of an attorney

____ e. other (explain)_____

Analogue #6

Your twenty-year-old adopted daughter has, with your knowledge, been successful in locating her birth parents. They are very needy people whose beliefs and values are very different from yours. Your daughter is attempting to maintain a friendship with her two younger biological half-sisters, who are teenagers. They borrow clothing from her that, if returned, is damaged and/or soiled. They call her to take them places when they don't have a ride. She loans them money that is never repaid. You do not approve of their friends, who are fast becoming your daughter's friends. What would you do?

___ a. forbid your daughter to see them

___ b. ask your daughter to go with your and your husband for family counseling

___ c. play it cool and hope your daughter's attraction to these people will pass

___ d. move out of state

___ e. other (explain)_____

Analogue #7

Your fourteen-year-old adopted son has met with his birth mother every six months since his birth and has developed a close relationship with her. One afternoon he comes to you and says, "You know, dad, I want to stay here with you, but I can't live with mom's rules. They are way out of line. I think I'd like to go live with Patty (birth mother). After all, she's my real mother."
You say, "_____

_____."

Analogue #8

Your eleven-year-old (adopted) son has just pitched a no-hit game and driven in three runs in their championship game. While you and the youngster are receiving accolades, a friend of yours makes the comment to you, "don't take too much of the credit yourself—after all, he has great genes going for him."

You feel like saying, "_____

_____."

You wind up saying, "_____

_____

_____."

Part 6

Please complete these statements:

1. I think the hardest part of adopting is _____

_____

_____.

2. The part of adoption I most fear is _____

_____

_____.

3. The way the media portrays adoption is _____

_____

_____.

_____
Number

INDIANA UNIVERSITY-PURDUE UNIVERSITY AT INDIANAPOLIS
INFORMED CONSENT STATEMENT

for

Project Title: A Study of Attitudes toward Current Adoption Agency Practices

INFORMATION

You are invited to participate in a research study, entitled "A Study of Attitudes Toward Current Adoption Agency Practices." The purpose of this study is to ascertain attitudes of prospective adoptive parents toward some of the newer practices in the field of adoptions. If you agree to participate, you will be one of approximately sixty subjects who will be participating in this research.

The expected duration of this study is 6-8 months.

The procedure involves the filling out of a questionnaire at home, which will take about 30-40 minutes of your time. Some of the items will involve the checking of a response to a particular question (i.e., the extent of agreement or disagreement to telling a child of his adoption to a three-year-old); other items will require a longer answer. Upon completion of the questionnaire, you will be asked to mail it back to the investigator. Upon its receipt, he may communicate with you by telephone to clarify some responses, as needed.

While all questionnaires are regarded as confidential, you should know that the investigator solely will be able to know the identity of each respondent. While agency personnel may know who is involved in the study, they will not know your individual response to any item, or group of items. If, by chance, you have an emotional reaction to any of the items, please feel free to contact the investigator. Your participation will not impact the agency decision to place a child with you in any way.

CONSENT

I have been given an opportunity to ask questions about this study; answers to such questions (if any) have been satisfactory.

The information in the study records will be kept confidential and will be made available only to persons conducting the study unless I specifically give my permission in writing to do otherwise. If the results of this study are published, I will not be identified.

If I have questions regarding the study I can reach Dr. Jerome Smith. . . .

In consideration of all the above, I give my consent to participate in this research study. I understand that I may drop out of or be withdrawn from the study without fear of penalty.

I acknowledge receipt of a copy of this informed consent statement.

SUBJECT'S NAME___(Print)_____

SUBJECT'S SIGNATURE _____

SIGNATURE OF WITNESS _____

SIGNATURE OF INVESTIGATOR _____

DATE _____   Address_____
                               City_____
                               Telephone (   ) _____

Bibliography

Allen, M. J. *Introduction to Psychological Research.* Itasca, Ill.: F. E. Peacock Publishers, 1995.

Anderson, S., M. Piantanida, and M. Anderson. "Normal Processes in Adoptive Families." In *Normal Family Processes,* ed. Froma Walsh. New York: Guilford Press, 1993.

Aumend, S., and M. C. Barrett. "Self-Concept and Attitudes toward Adoption: A Comparison of Searching and Non-Searching Adult Adoptees." *Child Welfare* 63 (May-June 1963): 251-259.

Bachrach, C. A., K. S. Stolley, and K. A. London. "Relinquishment of Premarital Births: Evidence from National Survey Data." *Family Planning Perspectives* 24, no. 1 (January-February 1992): 27-32.

Baran, A., and R. Pannor. "It's Time for a Sweeping Change." In commentary, *American Adoption Congress.* Summer 1990.

———. "Open Adoption as Standard Practice." *Child Welfare* 63 (May-June 1984): 245-250.

———. "Open Adoption." In *The Psychology of Adoption,* ed. D. M. Brodzinsky and M. Schechter. New York: Oxford University Press, 1990.

Barth, Richard, "Adoption Research: Building Blocks for the Next Decade." *Child Welfare* 73 (September-October 1994): 624-638.

Bartholet, Elizabeth. *Family Bonds: Adoption and the Politics of Parenting.* Boston: Houghton Mifflin Co., 1993.

Belbas, N. "Staying in Touch: Empathy in Open Adoptions." *Smith College Studies in Social Work* 57 (1987): 184-198.

Benson, P. L., et al. *Growing Up Adopted.* Minneapolis: Search Institute, 1994.

Bernstein, R. "Are We Still Stereotyping the Unmarried Mother?" In *The Unwed Mother,* ed. R. Roberts, New York: Harper and Row, 1963.

Berry, M. "The Effects of Open Adoption on Biological and Adoptive Parents and the Children: The Arguments and the Evidence." *Child Welfare* 70 (November-December 1991): 637-651.

————: "Risks and Benefits of Open Adoption." In *The Future of Children*. Los Altos, Calif.: Center for the Future of Children, The David and Lucile Packard Foundation, 1993, 125-138.

Blanton, R. L., and J. Deschner. "Biological Mothers' Grief: The Postadoptive Experience in Open versus Confidential Adoption." *Child Welfare* 69 (November-December 1990): 525-535.

Bradshaw, John. *Family Secrets: What You Don't Know Can Hurt You*. New York: Bantam Books, 1995.

Brinich, Paul M. "Adoption from the Inside Out: A Psychoanalytic Perspective." In *The Psychology of Adoption,* eds. David Brodzinsky and Marshall Schechter, New York: The Oxford Press, 1990.

Brinich, P. M., and E. Brinich. "Adoption and Adaptation." *Journal of Nervous and Mental Disease* 170 (1982): 489-493.

Brodzinsky, D. M. "Long-Term Outcomes in Adoption." In *The Future of Children*. Los Altos, Calif.: Center for the Future of Children, The David and Lucile Packard Foundation, 1993, 153–166.

————. "A Stress and Coping Model of Adoptive Adjustment." In *The Psychology of Adoption,* eds. D. M. Brodzinsky and M. D. Schechter, New York: Oxford University Press, 1990.

Brodzinsky, David M., Anne V. Gormly, and Sueann Ambron. *Lifespan Human Development*. New York: Holt, Rinehart, and Winston, 1986.

Brodzinsky, D. M., and Marshall Schechter, ed. *The Psychology of Adoption*. New York: Oxford University Press, 1990.

Brodzinsky, D. M., L. M. Singer, and A. M. Braff. "Children's Understanding of Adoption." *Child Development* 55 (1984): 869-878.

Brodzinsky, D. M., M. D. Schechter, and Robin Henig. *Being Adopted: The Lifelong Search for Self*. New York: Doubleday, 1992.

Chapman, C., P. Dorner, K. Silber, and T. Winterberg. "Meeting the Needs of the Adoption Triangle through Open Adoption: The Birth Mother." *Child and Adolescent Social Work* 3 (1986): 203-213.

Cline, F. "Special Parenting and Therapeutic Tricks." Paper presented at Psychiatric Institute Conference, Post Adoptive Placement Services—An Overview: The Need for Specialized Services. Fort Worth, Tex., April 1987.

Cocozelli, C. "Predicting the Decision of Biological Mothers to Retain or Relinquish Their Babies for Adoption: Implications for Open Placement." *Child Welfare* 68 (January-February 1989): 33-44.

Curtis, Jamie L. *Tell Me Again About the Night I Was Born*. New York: HarperCollins. 1996.

DeBoer, Robby. *Losing Jessica*. New York: Doubleday, 1994.

Erikson, E. *Childhood and Society*. New York: W. W. Norton, 1963.

Freud, A. *Psychoanalytic Study of the Child 13*. New York: International Universities Press, 1958.

Gold, Michael. *And Hannah Wept: Infertility, Adoption, and the Jewish Couple.* Philadelphia: The Jewish Publication Society, 1988.

Grabe, Pamela V., ed. *Adoption Resources for Mental Health Professionals.* New Brunswick, N.J.: Transaction Publishers, 1990.

Gritter, J. *Adoption Without Fear.* San Antonio: Corona, 1989.

Gross, H. E. "Open Adoption." A Research-Based Literature Review and New Data." *Child Welfare* 72 (May-June 1993): 269-284.

Grow, L., and D. Shapiro. *Black Children, White Parents.* New York: Child Welfare League of America, 1974.

Henshaw, S. K., and J. VanVort. "Abortion Services in the United States, 1987 and 1988." In *Family Planning Perspectives* 22 (May-June 1990): 102-108.

Jaffee, Benson, and David Fanshel. *How They Fared in Adoption.* New York: Columbia University Press, 1970.

Johnston, Patricia Irwin. *Adopting after Infertility.* Indianapolis, Ind.: Perspectives Press, 1992.

Jones, E. "On Transracial Adoption of Black Children." *Child Welfare 51* (March 1972): 156-164.

Kadushin, A., and J. Martin. *Child Welfare Services.* New York: Macmillan, 1988.

Kerlinger, Fred. *Foundations of Behavioral Research:* San Francisco: Holt, Rinehart and Winston, 1964.

Kirk, H. D. "Community Sentiments in Relation to Adoption." Ph.D. dissertation, Cornell University, 1953.

Kirk, H. David. *Adoptive Kinship.* Toronto: Butterworths, 1981.

———. *Looking Back, Looking Forward: An Adoptive Father's Sociological Testament.* Indianapolis, Ind., 1995.

———. *Shared Fate.* New York: The Free Press, 1964.

Komar, Miriam. *Communicating with the Adopted Child.* New York: Walker and Co., 1991.

Kowal, K. A., and K. M. Schilling. "Adoption through the Eyes of Adult Adoptees." *American Journal of Orthopsychiatry* 55 (July 1985).

Kraft, A. D., et al. "Some Theoretical Considerations on Confidential Adoptions. Part I: The Birth Mother." *Child and Adolescent Social Work* 2 (1985): 13-21.

———. "Some Theoretical Considerations on Confidential Adoptions, Part III: The Adopted Child." *Child and Adolescent Social Work Journal* 2 (Fall 1985): 139-153.

Kubler-Ross, E. *On Death and Dying.* New York: Macmillan, 1969.

Ladner, Joyce. *Mixed Families: Adopting across Racial Boundaries.* Garden City, N.Y.: Anchor/Doubleday, 1977.

———. "Should Whites Adopt Black Children." *Ebony,* December 1978.

Landers, Susan. "Adoption Agencies, Independents Vie." *NASW News* (November 1963).

Lawder, Elizabeth. *A Follow-up Study of Adoptions: Postplacement Functioning of Adoptive Families.* New York: Child Welfare League of America, 1969.

Lindsey, Jeanne. *Open Adoption: A Caring Option.* Buena Vista, Calif.: Morning Glory Press, 1987.

Littner, Ner. "The Natural Parents." Unpublished paper, 1956.

Loper, N. "A Companion Study of Personality Factors and Social Histories of Three Groups of Adopted Adults." Ph.D. dissertation, California School of Professional Psychology, Los Angeles, Calif., 1976.

Madison, Bernice. "Adoption: Yesterday, Today, and Tomorrow—Part I." *Child Welfare* 45 (May 1966): 253-268.

March, Karen. *The Stranger Who Bore Me: Adoptee-Birth Mother Relationships.* Toronto: Toronto Press, 1995.

Mason, Mary Martin. *Out of the Shadows: Birthfathers' Stories.* Edina, Minn.: O. J. Howard Publishing, 1995.

Mazor, Miriam. "Barren Couples." *Psychology Today,* May 1979, 101-108.

McKelvey, Carole A., and Jo Ellen Stevens. *Adoption Crisis: The Truth Behind Adoption and Foster Care.* Golden, Colo.: Fulcrum Publishing, 1994.

McRoy, R., H. Grotevant, and K. White. *Openness in Adoption.* New York Praeger, 1988.

McRoy, R., H. Grotevant, C. Elde, and D. Fravel. "Adoptive Family System Dynamics." *Family Process* 33 (June 1994): 125-146.

McRoy, R., and L. Zurcher. *Transracial and Inracial Adoptees.* Springfield, Ill.: Charles Thomas, Publisher, 1983.

Melina, Lois, and Sharon Roszia. *The Open Adoption Experience.* New York: Harper Perennial, 1993.

Norvell, M., and R. Guy. "A Comparison of Self-Concept in Adopted and Non-adopted Adolescents." *Adolescence* 12 (Fall 1977): 443-448.

Offer, D. *The Psychological World of the Teenager.* New York: Basic Books, 1969.

O'Neill, T. "Birth Father Rights." *Adoptive Families* (September-October 1994).

"Position Statement on Transracial Adoption." National Association of Black Social Workers, 1972.

Raymond, L. *Adoption and After.* New York: Harper and Row, 1955.

Reitz, M., and K. Watson. *Adoption and the Family System.* New York: The Guilford Press, 1992.

Ripple, Lilian. "A Follow-Up Study of Adopted Children." *Social Service Review* 42 (December 1968): 479-499.

Rosenberg, Elinor. *The Adoption Life Cycle.* New York: The Free Press, 1992.

Rosenthal, R., and R. L. Rosnow. *Essentials of Behavioral Research: Methods and Data Analysis.* New York: McGraw-Hill, 1991.

Scarnecchia, S. "Who Is Jessica's Mother? Defining Motherhood through Reality." *Journal of Gender and the Law* 3 (Fall 1994): 1-13.

Schechter, M. D., et al. "Emotional Problems in the Adoptee." *Archives of General Psychiatry* 10 (1964): 37-46.

Shapiro, C. "Sex Education and the Adoptive Family." *Social Work* 28 (July-August 1983): 291-296.

Shireman, Joan. *Growing Up Adopted.* Chicago: Child Care Society, 1988.

Siegel, D. H. "Open Adoption of Infants: Adoptive Parents' Perceptions of Advantages and Disadvantages." *Social Work* 38 (January 1993): 15-23.

Silverman, A., and Feigelman, W. *Chosen Children: New Patterns of Adoptive Relationships.* New York: Praeger, 1983.

Simon, R., and H. Altstein. *Transracial Adoption.* New York: John Wiley and Sons, 1977.

———. *Transracial Adoption: A Follow-Up.* Lexington, Ma.: Lexington books, 1981.

———. *Transracial Adoptees and Their Families: A Study of Identity and Commitment.* New York: Praeger, 1987.

Silber, Kathleen, and Patricia Dorner. *Children of Open Adoption.* San Antonio: Corona Publishing Co., 1990.

Smith, Jerome, and Franklin Miroff. *You're Our Child: The Adoption Experience.* Lanham, Md.: Madison Books, 1987.

Smith, Jerome. "Where Have We Come from, Where Are We Now, and Where Are We Going." Address given at Annual Program Meeting of National Council for Adoption (May 1995).

———. "Attitudes Toward the Sealed Record: An Empirical Study." In *You're Our Child: The Adoption Experience.* Lanham, Md.: Madison Books, 1987.

———. "Attitudes of Prospective Adoptive Parents toward Agency Adoption Practices, Particularly Open Adoption: Preliminary Empirical Findings." Paper presented at Annual Program Meeting of National Committee for Adoption (April 1991).

Smith, Sandra. "An Examination of Attitudes toward the Sealed Record." Presented to psychology class, North Central High School, Indianapolis, Ind., 1 May 1984.

Solnit, A., A. Freud, and J. Goldstein. *Beyond the Best Interests of the Child.* London: The Free Press, 1973.

Sorosky, A. D., A. Baran, and R. Pannor. "Identity Conflicts in Adoptees." *American Journal of Orthopsychiatry* 45 (January 1975): 18-27.

———. *The Adoption Triangle.* New York: Doubleday, 1984.

Standards for Adoption Service. New York: Child Welfare League of America, 1968.

Standards for Adoption Service. New York: Child Welfare League of America, 1988.

Stein, L. M., and J. L. Hoopes. *Identity Formation in the Adopted Adolescent.* New York: Child Welfare League of America, 1985.

Swenson, L. C. *Psychology and Law for the Helping Professions.* Pacific Grove, Calif.: Brooks/Cole Publishing Co., 1993.

Triseliotis, John. *In Search of Origins.* London: Routledge and Kegan Paul, 1973.

Ward, Margaret. "The Relationship between Parents and Caseworkers in Adoption." *Social Casework* 60 (February 1979): 96-103.

Watkins, Mary, and Susan Fisher. *Talking with Young Children about Adoption.* New Haven: Yale University Press, 1993.

Witmer, H., et al. *Independent Adoptions: A Follow-up Study.* New York: Russell Sage, 1963.

Young, L. *Out of Wedlock.* New York: McGraw-Hill, 1954.

Index

adopted adolescent, 89-99
  and open adoption, 98
  tasks to be achieved, 91-4
adoption as institutional response, 2
adoption definition, 1
adoption used as weapon, 31-2, 50,
  78, 87, 93-4
adoptive family development, 15
adoptive parent education, 12
attitudes towards adoption, 11
autobiographical account, 9-13, 71

"Baby Jessica," my role in, 121-
  130
"Baby Richard" case, 1, 5
biological chauvinism, 5
birth father movement, 6, 108
birth mothers, 110
  dealing with feelings, 111-19
  denial as a defense, 110-11
  head-heart reactions, 112
Brodzinsky, David M., 29, 42, 47,
  55, 70, 94, 126

changes in practice, 3-6, 7, 12, 35-
  36, 46, 102
counseling measures, 26, 96-7,
  110-13

decade of the 1970s, 6, 102

decreasing number of available
  infants, 4
dialogues
  with adolescent, 99
  with adult adoptee, 97-8
  with latency-aged child, 78-87

entitlement, the concept, 16-28, 55,
  71, 130
  applied to children, 28
  applied to parents, 16-9
  cases of entitlement failure, 18-
  9
  differentiated from claiming, 16
  related to unresolved mourning
  process, 19-22
Erikson, Erik, 70, 91-2
experts' views of openness, 42-3

fantasies, 84
feelings evoked, 76-7, 85, 87-8

heredity/environment interplay,
  136
historical development, 2-3

identification with parent figures,
  73-7, 95, 133
identity, 75-6, 94-5
infertility, 10, 22

Kubler-Ross stages, 22
working through feelings, 22-5

Kadushin, 6, 40, 42
Kirk, H. David, 11, 27, 52

loss, xiii-xiv, 9, 70

methodological considerations, 46-
51, 71
biased samples, 51, 57
probability theory, 49-50
randomness in sampling, 48-9
sampling theory, 48
McRoy, Ruth, 36, 58-60, 104
myths in adoption, 3-4, 74

National Association of Black
Social Workers, 6, 36, 102-3

openness continuum, 6, 36-7, 38-
44, 58, 100, 120, 132, 134
summary of findings, 58-67

psychological parent concept, 71,
124-5

research in adoption, 45-55
gap between research and
practice, 5
methodological flaws, 47-8
sampling and probability
theory, 48-50
spuriousness of outcome and
adoptive status, 41, 72
summary of large scale study,
53
role clarification, 135-6

shift in locus of control, 38-9
Smith, Jerome, 38-9, 44, 60-6, 121-
30
Stanley v. Illinois, 108-9

telling, 29-33, 71, 77
in confidential placements, 29-
31
in open placements, 32-3
therapeutic letter to birth father,
117-18
transracial adoptions, 101-6
research findings, 103-5

University of Chicago, 12

value issues, 128-30

About the Author

Jerome Smith, Ph.D., has been an associate professor at the Indiana University School of social work for nearly twenty-five years. He played an integral role in the famous "baby Jessica" adoption case, testifying as the primary evaluator of the parent-child bond. He is the author, along with Frank I. Miroff, of *You're Our Child: The Adoption Experience* (Madison Books, 1987). He is a visiting lecturer at the Jane Addams College of Social Work at the University of Illinois in Chicago. Dr. Smith will retire from full-time teaching in 1997, but plans to continue to teach and provide counseling on adoption issues. The father of three children, two of whom are adopted, Dr. Smith resides in Indianapolis, Indiana.